MW01174053

th

Beat *the* **Man**

the **Man** *who* **Beat** *the* **Man**

F.B. André

Canadian Cataloguing in Publication Data
André, F.B. (Frank Brian), 1955-
The man who beat the man

ISBN 1-896300-29-4
I. Title.

PS8551.N3594M37 2000   C813'.6   C00-910691-X
PR9199.3.A498M36 2000

Editor for the Press: Thomas Wharton
Cover and interior design: Ruth Linka
Cover image: Robert Seidlitz
Author photograph: T. Brown

The author wishes to thank all the good people at NeWest Press for making this book possible and better. Special thanks to Bob Kroetsch, Thomas Wharton, and Ruth Linka.

Some of these stories, in slightly different form, have been previously published, The Upsetter, *Event*; Jump Up And Kiss You, *The New Quarterly*; Each One Teach One, *Alberta Rebound*; Bienvenue au Canada, *Caribbean New Wave*; jes grew, *West Coast Review*; Another World, *Alberta Culture Short Story Contest*.

THE CANADA COUNCIL | LE CONSEIL DES ARTS
FOR THE ARTS | DU CANADA
SINCE 1957 | DEPUIS 1957

Canadian   Patrimoine
Heritage   canadien

NeWest Press acknowledges the support of the Canada Council for the Arts and the Alberta Foundation for the Arts for our publishing program. We also acknowledge the financial support of the Government of Canada through the Book Publishing Industry Development Program (BPIDP) for our publishing activities.

NeWest Press
201–8540–109 Street
Edmonton, Alberta T6G 1E6
(780) 432-9427
www.newestpress.com

00 01 02 03 04   4 3 2 1

PRINTED AND BOUND IN CANADA

to Tricia, Jules and Carla

CONTENTS

THE MAN WHO BEAT THE MAN

IN MY BUSINESS, authenticity is everything. I'm in Collectibles. Memorabilia. I like to think of what I do as a kind of forensic detective work. When I am asked to authenticate an item, my method is to first try and establish a chronology for that item. What I have found is that the burden of proof is almost always carried along in the how that item got from there to here.

Today's here is White Rock, BC, a city about an hour outside of Vancouver.

Boxing memorabilia always has a market but I've never seen it like this. It's ridiculous. Collectors like my client, Mr. Henday, are bidding up even the most obscure of champions from the lower weight classes. But the big ticket in boxing is always with the heavyweights … so my thinking is that the item Mr. Henday is after has to be connected to a heavyweight champion.

I'm in the clubhouse of the White Rock Golf & Country Club. It's the sort of place that is unabashedly run for the benefit of its male members: underpriced scotch and overpriced food.

My contact's name is Alexander Darren Rankin.

I study each foursome as they enter the clubhouse; I'm trying to match Rankin to his business card. It says that he is a Financial Advisor and Consultant. My third scotch says that he is more than an hour late.

A noisy foursome settles up at the bar with a lot more acrimony than should be necessary. One of this group confers with the bartender, who points towards me.

He is no Alexander. And he is no Darren.

He is unmistakably an Al.

Al Rankin is not a Financial Advisor or any sort of Consultant. He is a land shark. The small-pond variety.

He's in his fifties. He wears the sort of high-waist white polyester pants that certain golfers insist on. What's left of his hair is in a dorsal fin comb-over. He tries but fails to camouflage his shark teeth with a mustache.

Al the land shark trolls across the clubhouse, and in one continuous motion he lights his cigarette, takes a gulp, fish eyes me up and down, and introduces himself.

"Leslie Evers?" He seems taken aback that I am a woman. I know Leslie can be misleading. But who did he think he was speaking to on the phone?

"I thought you were your secretary, ha-ha!"

This guy had me fly out to the coast, drive all the way out to White Rock, and then kept me waiting for over an hour in a cheesy clubhouse.

"Do you golf? It's not what you shoot but what you score, ha-ha!"

"Not for a living," I say.

The tone of my remark brings Rankin's head up from his drink; he studies me with his wide-angle fish stare.

"I don't have them with me. The gloves."

I immediately stand up. It's a well-known fact that sharks cannot bluff. And it is my professional opinion that the best way to deal with a shark is to leave its waters. At once.

"They're not here," Rankin quickly overtakes me. "They're at my girlfriend's."

I keep on walking. Men in their fifties shouldn't have 'girl-friends'.

"She lives with her mother."

I'm having trouble with that mental picture and with finding my rental car.

"Her mom lives in Vancouver."

"Vancouver? Why in hell did you make me drive all the way out here?"

"It's a bit delicate," Al the pond shark says.

Right then it dawns on me. "You don't have them, do you? You don't even own the gloves."

There is something about the Als of this world that I find very annoying. And I'm getting a real antsy feeling about this Al. I know I'll be out of pocket on expenses, but already I'm thinking, ah—to hell with it.

I'm rolling up the window on my rental when Al Rankin says the two most magic words in all of boxing.

"Muhammad Ali."

⌒

Al the pond scum keeps me waiting again. This time I'm in Vancouver, in the foyer of a house in Point Grey. And one more layer of subterfuge is peeled off. The gloves belong not to Al's girlfriend but to her mother.

And so does the house.

The house is grand enough to have a foyer. The girlfriend ushers me into the study.

The girlfriend is in her early to mid-thirties.

"What do you think of our weather? We call it the Wet Coast." The girlfriend only knows how to make small talk.

She is a bird. Chirp, flit, chirp. Suddenly she flaps right out of the room.

You have to have an instinct in my business for what you don't see. At first glance, the study seems very well appointed. There are some beautiful items; every piece of furniture is a genuine collectible. I know people who would commit serious bodily harm to own that Queen Anne chair.

But somehow the room seems out of balance. There are two fairly large bald spots where the carpet is noticeably brighter, and there is a fresh circle on the wallpaper above the mantle where a clock would be perfect.

I make a slow inspection of the adjoining rooms. In the formal dining room, there is a wonderful inlaid mahogany sideboard that contains only the barest of bones—enough china for three, perhaps four, complete settings.

The only evidence of sports memorabilia that I come across is back in the study. There, in a lovely Canadiana pine hutch that serves as a trophy case, someone by the name of Yvon Winifred Peltcher has had himself an outstanding amateur athletic career, mostly at McGill University. In the late 1930s, he starred in hockey, tennis, and rugby football. But no boxing.

Eventually I hear the girlfriend twittering. She and Al flank Mother as they try to steer her towards the settee.

I can't tell if Mother is shaky or just shaking them off. Mother chooses the Queen Anne chair.

Mother is a bagpipe full of hard angles and loose bones, sharp and pointedly in charge. Only when she is fully composed in her chair does she signal her daughter, who then cues Al.

Al has played this scene before. And he is even more than a little bit bored by it all. He coughs and hurries his line.

"Mrs. Charlotte Slater—Leslie Evers, ha-ha!"

"Alexander Rankin," Mother says with a weary patience, like a schoolteacher upbraiding a difficult adolescent. "You did not clearly state our guest's name. Or her business."

Al begins to repeat the introductions. But Mrs. Slater waves him off.

I have the same feeling you get in a job interview—where it's not the answers that matter so much as how earnestly you can present yourself.

"Leslie Evers. I own a business that specializes in evaluating and authenticating collectibles."

"Mr. Rankin believes that men collect but we women inherit," Mrs. Slater says. "Do you share those views?"

"Women live longer than men. So yes, of course, we do tend to inherit, Mrs. Slater," I say. "But it's my observation that collecting is one of those human things that cuts across everything: both sexes, all economic classes, and all cultures. Women collect as much and as often as men."

Mrs. Slater nods. She seems ready with a follow-up question, but an over-eager Al cuts her off.

"—Show her the gloves, Charlotte."

Mrs. Slater remains fixed in her chair. I follow her gaze from the bald spot above the mantle and over to her daughter's inadvertently nervous laugh.

"What time is it? Mr. Rankin?" Mrs. Slater's voice crackles like salt on ice.

"It's very late," Al says. "It's very, very late in the day, Charlotte."

"I think it is time for Mr. Rankin to leave," she turns to her daughter. "Will you see him out?"

"Charlotte," Rankin makes no attempt to leave. "Miss Evers is an expert," he says. "Show her the gloves. She can put an end to all of your worries."

Not all. Not by a long shot. I should have taken the airport turnoff on the way back from White Rock. I could be on a plane right now; I could be jetting away from this. I wouldn't have to see an old woman covering her eyes from what's missing and from what's in front of her.

"Mother," the daughter's voice is high and shrill. "Al's only trying his best to help us."

The old lady deflates; she slumps back in her chair.

That's enough for me. I have to leave.

Rankin catches up to me in the foyer.

"Do you know what the property taxes alone on a house like this are? She's going to lose it all."

"I don't want anything to do with this, Rankin."

Rankin does what sharks do best—he closes in, he keeps pressing. "She has Sonny Liston's gloves. From the first fight. The gloves Liston wore when Ali—Cassius Clay—took the title from him."

"Miss Evers?" The old lady herself has come after me.

"May I please have a word alone Miss Evers?"

DENVER, 1960

Nathan's gym in the Carl Joyner Building has an ever-present smell of carbolic soap, but nothing can mask the scent of desperation that pervades the dimly lit change rooms and the sparsely equipped workout area. A lone boxer is at work in the makeshift ring. He is throwing combinations that send phantom after phantom crashing to the canvas floor. He is Charles 'Sonny' Liston, the blackest man in all of America. The prototype for the "baddest man on the planet." An ex-convict with an arrest sheet as long as his famous reach. He is the possessor of the best left hand in all of boxing. A sinister figure, with a perpetual look of blood in his eyes.

The mile-high air in Denver is thin. And Liston is not in top shape; he labours to breathe. The floor of the ring is a thick mixture of his sweat and curls of sawdust.

Every so often, Liston stoops to examine his footwork: he is committing to memory the pathways of destruction that he has carved out in the sawdust.

A priest in his dress whites enters the gym from a side door and hurries up to the ring.

"Where's Apples?" The priest says. As if on cue, a squat black man appears, clanging two buckets.

One bucket holds fresh sawdust and the other water.

Apples slops some sawdust onto the canvas floor; the boxer greedily takes big gulps of the water.

"Don't you be stoppin' and coolin' yet, Sonny!"

Apples has cherub cheeks and an impossibly flat nose; his voice is high up on the register like a steam-kettle whistle.

Liston lifts the whole bucket to his lips and takes huge, grinning gulps.

"Sonny, no! Don't you be coolin'!" Apples tries to wrestle the bucket away, splashing himself and the priest in the process.

"Jeeze, I'm sorry, Father Murph," Apples apologizes.

"Cut it out, you two," Father Murphy checks the damage to his vestments, "I've got a wedding to do."

Apples casts his high-pitched appeal to Father Murph. "He's gotta train an' train right."

"Jersey Joe himself was here, Father." Apples says.

"Jersey Joe, he say Sonny has the best left he ever did see. And there be talk, serious talk, 'bout Jersey Joe himself, maybe the ref, for Sonny's title shot."

"—If'n I ever gets a shot."

"You'll get your shot, Sonny," the priest says. "And when that time comes you want to be ready in every way. Am I right?"

"Yes, Father Murph." Liston, who looks baleful even at the best of times, wears his longest hangdog look.

"Sonny, I've talked and talked to you enough about this," Father Murphy says. "I'll not be listening to any more nonsense excuses. I've made arrangements to help you with your reading and writing."

"I—I don't much like book learnin'." A downcast Liston enters a no-contest plea. "I started too old and now I'm too bone hard-headed for book learnin'."

"Jeezus! Sonny, weren't you payin' any attention at all to what Jersey Joe was sayin'?" Apples takes a fresh turn at riding Sonny. "Anytime you gets the chance to talk to a former champ, you better list'n up.

"Jersey Joe, he been to the top. Jersey Joe, he done been where you want to go." Apples presses his point. "Did you at least hear what Jersey Joe said 'bout the Bomber?"

The Bomber is Joe Louis. Apples knows that Joe Louis is Liston's idol.

"Yeah. I heard. Yeah."

"Well? You tell me. Sonny. What did he say?"

"Jersey Joe," Liston slips into the exact whiskey and raspberry voice of Jersey Joe. "People say how Joe Louis is a credit to the Negro race. The Bomber gets five dollars just for signaturin' his name on a piece of paper.

"The Bomber gets twenty dollars just for smilin'. If you take a picture of the Bomber and he put his arm aroun' you, you best leave at least a hundred in his kerchief pocket.

"Now ain't that," Liston grins, "the easiest money makin' you ever hear 'bout?"

"Jeezus Sonny," Apples pipes up. "Now ain't that a good green bejeezus reason for you to be learnin' how to read and write?"

"Apples," Father Murphy says, "I'll be thanking you not to be taking the good Lord's name in vain."

"Jee—Sorry, Father Murph." Apples makes his apology into the water bucket.

"Sonny, I'll set up a schedule," Father Murphy says, "to help you with your reading and writing. You've got to treat it just like your training. Pay attention. And don't be giving off any more of your guff."

Sonny Liston makes no reply.

"Do you hear me?" Father Murphy insists on confirmation from Sonny.

"Yes, Father Murph."

"Good. I've got to be going. I've got a wedding to do. And from the looks of the bride," Father Murphy winks, "I'll be doing a baptism soon."

Sonny grins. He extends his left hand straight and pulls the shotgun trigger with his right. It's uncanny how Sonny does it. He makes the exact sound of a shotgun rifle going off.

~

"Yvon was my first husband."

Mrs. Slater's bony fingers pry open the trophy case. She takes out a large cigarbox. The gloves are stuffed with tissue paper and crammed into the box.

"We met at McGill. Yvon was in Engineering. And I was in Education. I wasn't too sure about teaching but in those days it was either Teacher or Nurse.

"We both signed up. It was the right thing to do. We got married before Yvon was sent overseas. I was supposed to go overseas as well, but I didn't. I served as a wireless operator in Halifax.

"We both did our bit willingly. But when it was over, those bloody fools in the army fumbled Yvon's official release. It cost him his job at McGill. And to this day, I still think he got shabby treatment from McGill. But you could never ever get Yvon to say a bad word about McGill. Not him."

While Mrs. Slater is back in wartime Montreal, I take a good look at the gloves. They've picked up the smell of cured tobacco. The leather is quite stiff with some minor cracking, the seams are all okay, the lacing is okay. The gloves are in good to excellent shape.

"Forgive me, Miss Evers," Mrs. Slater circles back to the present. "People my age—we use the war like a divider for every important thing."

"It's quite all right, Mrs. Slater." I smile and say that I understand, that my dad was in the war too.

"Mrs. Slater," I gently jog her back. "So how did your husband gain possession of the gloves?"

"Oh no, my dear," Mrs. Slater says, "you misunderstood. The gloves are mine."

"You? You and Sonny Liston? You knew Liston?"

There is no way to hide my surprise.

"Yes, we met in Denver. That's where I met my Bertie. My second husband, Bertram Slater. He was a geologist, a widower and a Canadian like me, so everybody thought we'd be a good match."

I'm trying, but I can't put together a picture of this drying white rose, this thorny old woman, and Sonny Liston.

"Mrs. Slater, in order to authenticate this item I'll need chapter and verse. Tell me exactly—when and where did you first meet Sonny Liston?"

"The Loyola Catholic, in Denver. We had Loyolas in Montreal; that's why I went to them in Denver."

"You met Sonny Liston in church?" I am now convinced that

Mr. Henday has not only sent me on a wild goose chase, but that I've actually caught the goose.

"Not in church. Through Father Murphy. He was a Jesuit. They always have their logical reasons. The Jesuits.

"Father Murphy," Mrs. Slater smiles, "he was a lovely man. He kept an open room in his heart for people like Charles."

"And when was this?"

"I first met Charles in 1960. I know it was 1960. Because it was exactly one year after my Yvon passed."

DENVER, 1960

Charlotte Peltcher waits with rising unease at the back of a smelly old gym for Father Murphy to come and introduce her to her prospective student. He did tell her that her student is a prizefighter. But he neglected to mention that he is a Negro. She knows next to nothing about boxing and less than nothing about Negroes.

Three Negroes are in a boxing ring at one end of the gym. One hulking Negro is sparring with another smaller Negro. The third Negro is screaming the same high-pitched instructions over and over.

"Go inside! Jab downtown! Now hook upstairs!"

Charlotte Peltcher watches with a mixture of horror and repulsion as the smaller man is battered about, until he is cornered.

The third Negro is now shouting, "That's enough! Jeezus, Sonny! That's enough!"

The bigger Negro keeps on pounding until his opponent crumbles to the floor. He stands over and glares down at the beaten man.

The third man comes between and helps steer the fallen man away. The beaten man spits out his mouthpiece and hurls his headgear as he quits the ring.

At that moment, Charlotte Peltcher also decides to quit the gym. She turns and runs into the good Jesuit shepherd, Father Edward Murphy.

Father Murphy has to call on all of his Jesuit training in rhetoric and logic to get her to calm down.

"Charlotte," Father Murphy finds his winning argument with a simple appeal to conscience. "If we can't even give someone a first chance … how are we ever going to be able to do what Jesus asks of us?"

~

"Jeezus, Sonny, when I say stop—you stop." Apples' high pipe of a voice is like a drill sergeant's whistle. "You think it's so easy to get you sparring partners way up here in Denver?"

"What do you care, Apples?" Liston sulks off.

"No, Sonny, no. Sonny, you know it ain't like that." Apples tries to explain as he follows Liston around the ring. Liston keeps his broad back to him. "Come on, Sonny," Apples pleads. "You know it ain't like that."

Liston about-turns suddenly, "You're quittin' on me, Apples. How can you just quit on me just like that?"

Apples shakes his head in vigorous denial.

Liston's eyes are full of blood and the need to hurt.

"The first smell of money and—bam! You're gone. You think I need you? Apples, I don't need you."

But he does. Liston's fists are so big; he always has extra tape and double-knot lacing on his gloves. Liston bites at the lacing. Apples moves forward to help him; an angry Liston shoves him away.

Apples tries again; he closes the space between them, firmly takes hold of one of Liston's gloves, and begins to peel off the tape.

Liston fidgets like a child getting his shoelaces done up.

"Hold still," Apples admonishes him. "Sonny, I have to step aside. I'm in your way now. Blinky says Carbo wants you back in Philly, training with Tocco. Tocco will take good care of you."

"Apples, I—"

"—Jeezus, Sonny. Can't make it any plainer than that. Carbo pulls the strings. Carbo don't want me handlin' you. I leave, you move up. You gets your shot."

"I don't want it this way," Liston says. "I want you there, Apples," Liston stubbornly insists. This time it's Apples who shoves him and takes an angry step back.

"Nobody cares what you or I want, Sonny." Apples' high voice becomes a raw hiss. "You list'n up good Sonny! We're in America. And we're niggers. You do whatever it takes to gets your shot."

Apples resumes work on peeling off Sonny's gloves.

"You're ready, Sonny. Jeeze, you are so ready. Not much more I can show you nohow. It's all comin' down to you and that Floyd Patterson."

"That pretty boy," Liston's grunt is a dismissal, "he's a dog."

"Pretty boy Floyd is gonna run from you like a dog with his

tail 'tween his legs." Apples sets the scene. "You'll beat the black off him so bad, he be yipp'n for his mama."

"Yippin' for his mama," Sonny chuckles as he echoes Apples. "I'll bust his butt so hard his dog tail'll come pop right out his head."

"And then," Apples sows another seed, "you'd be the man."

"I'd be the man." Liston nods. "For a fact, I'd be the heavy-weight champion of the whole entire world."

"For a fact," Apples agrees as he pulls off both gloves now and raises Sonny's arms in the universal salute of all champions. Liston parades about the ring with his arms aloft, dreaming, willing the moment into focus.

"When you the champ," Apples follows close, in step, in Sonny Liston's shadow.

"When you the man who beat the man, no one can ever take that away from you."

⁓

"Father Murphy tells me you're from the South?" Charlotte Peltcher opens with the little that she knows about him. "I'm from Canada, myself. Rosemere, a little town near Montreal, Quebec."

Liston is as impassive as a rock.

"I'm not, strictly speaking, an English teacher." Her qualification draws no response from Liston. "But I've been a teacher for fifteen years, mostly junior high." Sonny Liston's eyes are full of blood; he makes no attempt to meet hers. He is still sweating from his sparring session and his breathing fills the gym with steam. She cannot stand the stale sweat and soap smell in here, and she can't think of any reason why she should be anywhere near to the most frightening man she has ever seen. He is well over six feet tall; he is wearing only an awful scowl and his boxing trunks. The muscles in his arms and shoulders are massive; his upper torso looks like it belongs on a machine. Even his silence is fierce.

Charlotte is too scared to up and leave. Sonny is wishing that she would just plain go away. He is still full of raw, fidgety energy from his workout; he assumes his fighting stance and throws combinations at the shadows.

"How long have you been a boxer?" Charlotte tries again.

"Depends," Sonny says, "on what you mean. Been a fighter all my life. All's I know is fightin'. But I only been a boxer for a few years. I only learned how to box in prison. Ain't much else to do in the joint, exceptin' train."

Father Murphy neglected to mention prison; it's Charlotte turn for a long, stony silence. She watches him shadowbox. There is something compelling and graceful in his movements; she cannot reconcile it with the savagery that she witnessed earlier in the ring.

"You have absolutely the longest arms," Charlotte blurts out. She can't believe she just said that.

Sonny extends his arms to their fullest span; he looks down the barrel of each of his arms in turn, in mock surprise, as if noticing them for the first time himself. He closes his stance, his hands held high now, protecting his face.

"You really think you can learn me somethin' 'bout readin' an writin'?"

Charlotte looks into the blood-red eyes peering out from behind the huge fists, behind the question.

"Oh yes," Charlotte nods. She laughs a high, nervous bird-song laugh.

Sonny grins, and he mimics her laugh exactly.

～

"I'll admit," Mrs. Slater leans forward to confide, "that when I first met Charles I was repulsed by his fighting. If it wasn't for Father Murphy, I would have turned away."

Mrs. Slater settles back in her Queen Anne chair.

It's hard to get a good read on her. Her eyes have that cloudy milk quality that comes with age.

Her story is all hot air, a huge balloon. It's common knowledge that Liston was illiterate all his life. A couple of quick punctures and I'm on my way to Vegas.

"So, Mrs. Slater," I say. "You taught Sonny Liston how to read and write?"

"Oh my heavens, no." Mrs. Slater cocks her head to one side and gives a light bird-song laugh. I see where and how her daughter gets some of her mannerisms.

"Charles was not my best student. He was a wonderful mimic and he had a good memory, but he was very insecure. If he had applied himself a bit more, I'm positive he could have mastered reading and writing."

"The next time was quite a bit better," Mrs. Slater continues. "Charles at least learned how to make his own signature in a fairly confident fashion."

"The next time?" My quick math says that this was what? Nearly forty years ago, in the sixties, in black and white America? It just doesn't add up.

"How many times did you meet Liston?"

Mrs. Slater takes offense at my tone.

"Charles and I were friends. It wasn't a common thing then," Mrs. Slater goes straight to the root of my doubt, "but is it still so hard to accept?"

"Excuse me Mrs. Slater," I soft-pedal. "I have to be very precise in my kind of work."

"I don't understand," Mrs. Slater says, "why these gloves should have such a tremendous value?"

"Potential value, Mrs. Slater," I quickly correct.

The gloves sit in her lap like dark, ripe plums.

"Al says that these gloves are worth thousands, in the tens of thousands. What do you think is the potential value of these gloves, Miss Evers?"

Al's been doing his homework.

"What these gloves are worth is between the buyer and the seller. I'm already working for someone who wants an opinion on their authenticity. You should get an independent appraisal."

"I see," says Mrs. Slater.

But I don't know if she really does. Collectibles are entirely subjective. How can a baseball card that came free with a penny's worth of gum be worth over half a million dollars?

If, if these are the gloves that Sonny Liston wore for his title defense against Cassius Clay, then they are a direct link in a coveted chain. The heavyweight championship of the world has a lineage. There is a true line that runs right back to the first champion. Any item that is directly linked to a champion takes on added significance, to collectors like Mr. Henday, such items are highly prized.

Muhammad Ali has a special place: he is far and away the brightest star in the sky. Any item connected to Ali draws a huge premium. The gloves of the man he beat are forever linked to Ali's moment of ascendancy.

I like my evidence to be a lot more concrete. I like facts that I can verify. My reputation is my livelihood. There is no way, on the strength of what Mrs. Slater has given me so far, that I could or would authenticate the gloves. But Mr. Henday is obsessive, he is compulsive, and he is very rich. And if I were the one sitting in that Queen Anne chair, I would start the bidding at six figures.

For that kind of money, people can be very inventive.

For that kind of money, I want hard proof.

"When did you first gain possession of the gloves?"

"1964." Mrs. Slater says without hesitation. "It was just before we moved back to Canada."

So far I've got Who, What, When, and Where from her.

"Why did Liston give you his gloves?" I ask.

Mrs. Slater is quiet for a long moment. Long enough for me to think about posing the question again.

Al and the daughter enter.

A beaming, a solicitous Al, cannot contain or hide his greedy excitement.

"Why would Liston give you his gloves?" I ask again.

"I took them." Mrs. Slater laughs her bird-song laugh. "I took these gloves away from him."

The daughter and Al do a pantomime of close concern around Mrs. Slater.

"Charlotte," Al's been listening at the keyhole, "I'll arrange for an appraiser. I'll get you the best in the business."

"Thank you so much for your time, Miss Evers," Mrs. Slater says.

A school bell might as well ring: dismissed.

LAS VEGAS

Vegas is the perfect place to get a divorce. Losing out and letting go are somehow easier to swallow in better-luck-next-time Vegas. I wish I could have gotten my divorce in Vegas; I would have liked to have had one perfect thing to take from my marriage.

I'm always glad to be in Vegas. I'm in love with nighttime Vegas—the moon in a desert sky full of possibilities. I even like the gaudy, over-the-top neon come-ons along the strip. And I like how the soft lighting and two-way mirrors inside the casinos can make everyone look both thin and greedily attractive.

Unfortunately, this is daytime Vegas. The sky is a blue headache and the sun is as hot as a hangover in hell.

"Sonny got the full Vegas sendoff, Miss Evers. I was working with the Inkspots. Man oh man, when we sang "O Sonny Boy," *a capella*, if you please, wasn't a dry eye left in the whole damn desert."

"—Rosie Russell! The way you telling it, make it sound like you were lead singer! Miss Evers, he no Inkspot, he no singer.

He was a roadie for the 'Spots is all. You gots to take everything Rosie say with salt. And aspirin."

Yolanda Carrick muscles Rosie aside and takes up her rightful station at centre stage. After all, she's the one that owns the gloves.

Yolanda Carrick is the granddaughter of Conrad 'Apples' Johnson. She dresses ten years younger and twenty pounds tighter than she should.

"I don't much remember my grandpa," Yolanda says. "But I heard him tell the story of how he got these gloves often enough."

Yolanda hands over the gloves. They're pretty much identical to the pair in Vancouver. Not as well cared for, but still in good shape.

"Grandpa got them from Sonny Liston himself. The very same night he got beat and lost the crown."

"—My man Muhammad," Rosie cuts in, "whupped his ass."

"Rosie, you don't know squat. My grandpa always swore that Sonny Liston coulda whupped Ali's ass, but Liston didn't train proper for that fight."

"Yeah," Rosie rebuts, "history don't lie. How come Ali whupped his butt even worse in the next fight?"

Yolanda is out of ammo.

"All I know is that these be the gloves, Miss Evers."

"Is there some way you can verify your grandfather's story, Miss Carrick?" I ask.

"Nobody never thought that there was anything important about the gloves." Yolanda shrugs. "They were just part of grandpa's stuff. He kept a lot of stuff to do with boxing."

"Old Apples," Rosie adds, "Up until a few years ago he was still teaching kids how to box. They say he had peculiar ideas about training. They say how he was deep into the psychology side of boxing. They say he was way ahead of his time."

"Wait," Yolanda says. "I remember my grandpa used to say that Toco knew. I don't know who this Toco is."

"Tocco," I say, "is dead."

Dead. Dead ends.

Mr. Henday is going to have to hunt for confirmation for his next treasure someplace else. And it looks like I made a bad call by opting for a percentage on contingency of sale. "Miss Carrick," I say. "Why don't you tell it to me again. From the top."

CHICAGO, 1962

Conrad 'Apples' Johnson, is cap in hand hesitating outside the champion's dressing room, wondering what his part in the celebration should be.

Sonny sent him a ticket.

Sonny wanted him there.

Jeezus would have to be roasting in hell; nothing could have kept Apples away. No way no how could he miss seeing Sonny get his shot.

Apples wedges his way into the dressing room.

"You the man! You the champ!" Apples' falsetto is added to and lost in the excitement—corks popping, flashbulbs and microphones, all asking, "How does it feel? Feel?"

The taste of victory is sweet in Sonny's mouth. And along

with victory comes this dreamed-about, this hoped-for, this new-found thing: respect.

"Champ? Champ? How do you feel about the South?"

Sonny Liston turns to the question, unsure about what's being asked.

"How do you feel about the civil rights movement? The marches down south? Are you going to join the marchers?"

Sonny Liston is stunned that someone would ask for his opinion about something like that. And amazed when they hang on to his every word.

"I ain't got no bulletproof ass," Liston gives his droll response.

"Apples? Apples!" Liston spots a familiar face. And he comes right over to embrace, to include him.

"I told you I'd bust his tail. I beat Floyd like a dog. He was shittin' scared from the git-go. I knew I had him from before the bell.

"Apples, you gotta come back to Philly with me," Sonny invites him to share in his spotlight. "I'm gonna be gettin' me a ticker-tape parade. Gonna show the whole world who be the man. Who be the new—"

Apples has time for only one word, half a word, before the swell of new fame sweeps Sonny away.

"—Champ."

DENVER, 1963

Charlotte Peltcher is about to scandalize her Denver neighbours, again.

This time in broad daylight.

Two carloads of Negroes. Loud and boisterous Negroes, all in the same uniform of red and black track suits with 'Liston' in white letters across the back—an embroidered entourage playing follow their leader's picket fence grin into Charlotte Peltcher's backyard for a cookout, her French Canadian cooking coming mighty close to Louisiana Creole, a celebration in honour of the one, the only, the true heavyweight champion of the whole entire world.

Father Edward Murphy arrives. He is swallowed up like cream in coffee.

Apples and Sonny are in a heated, hot-versus-cold debate over the merits of Charlotte's fried chicken.

"I've been eatin' Miss Charlotte's fried chicken for two, three years," is Sonny's basic argument. "I know what I'm talkin' 'bout here, Apples."

"You done been eatin' the poor woman out of house and home," Apples razzes him back. "Sonny, you eat so dang fast your poor mouth still hopin' for you to belch so it can see what the food was like."

"Charlotte," Father Murphy checks up on Sonny's progress, "has he been practicing?"

Her answer is a shrug and a laugh as light as bird song.

"You could be the next Charles Dickens," Father Murphy takes his turn at Sonny, "if you put as much effort into your reading and writing as you do your eating."

"Ain't that the truth!" Apples looks to Miss Charlotte for agreement.

Miss Charlotte is the stir spoon in this swirling company of men, as she bubbles from kitchen to backyard, dishing out and soaking up glad laughter. And when the celebration winds down, day into evening, two carloads into one small circle around her kitchen table, Charlotte has her big news to share. His name is Bertram—Bertie Slater, and he makes her happy.

"Bertie Slater is a good man," Father Murphy allows, "even though he's of the wrong faith."

"Where's this man Bertie?" Sonny asks in a low growl. "I want to look him over."

Charlotte shies around the question; she knows the answer is that her Bertie is a lot more than a little uneasy around Negroes.

"If this Bertie man ever give you any trouble…" Sonny scowls, his famous bloody scowl.

"Will you come to rescue me, Charles?" Charlotte has learned to look past the blood in Sonny's eyes. Apples also sees right through him. "You gonna call out your Geraldine to take care of Bertie man?"

Geraldine is Sonny's wife. Sonny lives in mortal fear of her.

Sonny turns his bloody glare on Apples but he can't hold it; he begins to laugh, a deep, infectious laughter that they all join in.

Apples is glad to at least hear Sonny laughing again. Sonny hasn't been the same since he got back from Philly. Apples detects something broken or denied.

Sonny Liston never got his ticker-tape parade. Philadelphia never embraced him. Never gave him a champion's welcome. After that one magical night of victory he was once again type-cast as villain.

Sonny Liston wanted so much to be a hero, like his hero, The Bomber.

'Joe Louis is a credit to the Negro race.' Sonny desperately wanted for people to say that about him. But Sonny never got more than a single taste of the automatic respect that went to the champion. And with that respect came an entitlement: Sonny never got what he was truly fighting for—his right to a second chance.

Hunger and rage are enough to propel a fighter when he's up and coming, but Apples well knows that a champion must fight from a different perspective.

A champ doesn't just fight to keep what he has.

A champ defends what he has become.

MIAMI BEACH, 1964

> *Sonny Sonny you're a fatty*
> *You can't hit me you can't catch me*
> *You're too slow—I'm too fast*
> *I'm the future ... you're the past*

The new champion demonstrates the shuffle. No one has ever danced in such perfect lock-step with fame as Muhammad Ali. He is holding court in his dressing room, fame's new oasis.

Sonny Liston's dressing room is a desert.

Liston is slumped on a bench; his eyes are bruised and bloodier than ever, and his left shoulder is badly dislocated.

Apples gingerly tests the shoulder; Sonny winces but says nothing.

Apples holds his tongue. He gave every warning he could before the fight. No one took Clay seriously. Not Tocco, not

Carbo, and least of all not Sonny. Apples applies some ointment and does some patching on Sonny's bruised face.

"The fresh fool was talkin' the whole time." Liston says. "The whole fight. He's talkin'."

"Jeeze," Apples nods, "that Clay boy's a nutcase."

"Rhymin' fool," Sonny mutters to himself.

Quickest heavyweight I've ever seen though, Apples thinks, as he helps Sonny with his gloves. Apples carefully unwinds the yards of tape until the laces are exposed, then he loosens the double knots and gently eases the gloves off.

Sonny tries to stand. He still can't get his feet going right. Sonny wobbles over to the urinal. He's spitting and peeing blood. Shaking his head all the while.

Apples is shaking his head too as he packs up Sonny's gear. Any fighter will have to be at his peak, both mentally and physically, to beat young Mr. Clay.

"Sonny, when you ready to train, and I mean train right and proper," Apples closes the gym bag, "I'll be in Vegas."

~

Mr. Henday will listen eagerly to my report. But in the end he will hear only what he wants to hear. He is a collector.

Yolanda Carrick has a fairly direct link to the item. Her grandfather was Liston's trainer at different times. When Liston lost the title, Conrad 'Apples' Johnson was working as a spotter in Liston's camp. Johnson's job was to spy on Ali in training. Television footage confirms that on the night of the fight, Johnson was a part of Liston's entourage.

I cannot verify Mrs. Slater's claim either. I'm not even sure her gloves are for sale.

But Mr. Henday is a man with way too much money. And I know what Mr. Henday will say to that. Leslie dear, everything has its price.

Who do I believe?

I've given that very question a fair bit of thought.

Yolanda Carrick and Rosie Russell are small-time Vegas. If Mr. Henday were to offer them five grand, they'd immediately ask for twenty, hoping to get ten. But if Mr. Henday offered them five hundred dollars, they'd settle for that and the chance to sell him any other old thing left behind by her grandfather.

Al Rankin swims in different waters. He has caught the scent of a big score. But I don't think he or the girlfriend have the smarts between them to concoct something elaborate like this.

It comes back to Mrs. Slater. There's no doubt that she really needs the money. I can't help feeling that somewhere in that drafty old house she must have the proof that would establish her friendship with Liston. And her ownership of the gloves.

Mrs. Slater never did explain. Why?

I would like it to be Mrs. Slater; it would be a much bigger sale and my commission would be a whole lot better.

I'm telling Mr. Henday that I'm taking another trip out to Vancouver.

DENVER, 1964

Charlotte Slater enters the gym; her eyes adjust to the low light, but her nose refuses to accept the carbolic soap. Two bantam-weight roosters are preening about the makeshift ring. Four nearly naked, over-muscled young men barely glance up at her before resuming the lesson in their destructive trade on the heavy bags.

Charlotte sees no sign of Sonny. She heads towards the change rooms.

"Hello Charles."

"Miss Charlotte," Sonny takes a welcome break from scowling and from packing up his gear.

"Father Murphy tells me you're leaving?" Charlotte asks.

"Yeah. Goin' to Vegas. Gettin' ready for the rematch. Suppose to be in Vegas. Jersey Joe gonna be the ref for sure."

"You'll get to see Apples," Charlotte says.

"Sure enough," Sonny agrees. "When's you expectin'?" Sonny points to her protruding belly. "Old Bertie is a fast worker."

"We're moving, too," Charlotte pats her belly. "Back to Canada. My Bertie thinks there's too much trouble going on in America right now. What with the assassinations and everything. A fresh start will be best for all of us."

"Tell old Bertie he's right," Sonny nods in agreement. "A fresh start is the best thing. Tell old Bertie I'm comin' on up with you," Sonny chuckles. "Tell him the big old bear is comin' on up to Canada."

"Charles," Charlotte's smile says she knows all about his teasing and Bertie's fear of Negroes. "You know you're always welcome in my house."

"Miss Charlotte…" Sonny searches for the right way to say it. "All my born days, far back as I can remember, everybody I ever know, always been trying to beat somethin' outta me.

"Startin' with my pops. Lord he tried somethin' fierce.

"Even Father Murph," Liston grins, "he be forever tryin' to beat the devil outta me. But not you, Miss Charlotte. You only been trying to beat some good into me.

"Now, Father Murph, he done expected, he supposed to do some good. But you, Miss Charlotte, you been real generous."

"You don't have to thank me, Charles." Charlotte is touched by his sincerity.

"Miss Charlotte," Sonny has a feeling about this parting, "You is the onlyest body I ever met who never once try to get somethin' for nothin' from me."

"I have no intention of ever 'gettin' somethin' for nothin' from you," Charlotte mimics him. "But you've already put so much effort into it. I want you to promise me that you'll try and keep up with your reading and writing."

"Yes, Miss Charlotte. I'll try." Sonny finds it much easier to believe the lie.

"Thank you, Charles."

His friendship has come to mean a lot to her also. Father Murphy was right; tutoring Charles gave her a purpose when she needed some focus other than grief. But it has also provided her with something else: it has helped her across that fault line that has become the great divide. The thing that her Bertie fears most in an America of assassins and martyrs, is Us and Them. Charlotte has the for-sure knowledge that the most reviled and feared of Them all is this man who is fiercely loyal, who is funny and genuine, and who is having trouble packing up his gear.

"Here Charles," Charlotte offers. "Let me help you with that."

"Now there be somethin' else that I really do notice," Liston says in his usual droll way as he accepts her help. "An awful lot less people offer to help when you're *not* the champ."

Sonny slips on a pair of boxing gloves. He slaps them together, hard. Again and again.

"Old Apples," Sonny's voice rises to mimic that of Apples. "He say, 'Now these be the bejeezus gloves that cost you the title.'

"'Sonny!' Apples say. 'You wear these gloves every day. Sonny! You remember every punch, every mistake.'

"'And only when I'm done rememberin' everythin' I ever done wrong', Apples says, 'then we can start fresh.' Then he can train me proper so I can whup that fresh-mouth Clay.

"I don't want to cross Apples," Sonny says. "He know pretty near everthin' to know 'bout trainin'. But I'm sure sick and fed up with all the bad rememberin'.

"Been doin' that way too long.

"Been doin' that all my life.

"You know," Sonny makes his appeal directly to her, "I'm surely ready for a fresh start too, Miss Charlotte."

Miss Charlotte agrees. She does the only and best thing that she can think of; she snaps the gym bag shut.

"Come here Charles."

Charlotte reaches for the gloves. She pulls and works at them until the gloves come off his huge fists.

"Give these to me. If Apples makes so much as a fuss, you tell him I took them."

They leave the gym and come out into the cold Denver air. Miss Charlotte pulls her coat about her big belly and she uses the boxing gloves for mitts.

Charlotte looks at the gloves and slaps them together, again and again, like she's seen him do. It makes for a strange sight.

Sonny grins at her. He wears the look of a man who knows, for at least this one clear, bright Denver day, that he deserves a second chance.

THE UPSETTER

SOME SAY GRAVEYARDS.

Some prefer days.

On afternoons, I catch the bus for work in front of Robinson's.

The Bayfront bus is a cursor; it takes you on a loop through the circuitry of Hamilton. From Robinson's to the top of Burlington Street, the Bayfront gains on each exchange; two or three men board at each stop. Some carry rolled-up newspapers, some are armed with lunch pails, some head straight for empty seats with scarcely a nod to those they know, others plop themselves down besides fellow warriors and pick up exactly on yesterday's conversations that have been going on for years.

Once it gets onto Burlington, the Bayfront empties out twice as fast as it filled up. The spill of men is quickly swallowed up by giants.

At my stop, I check the time. I have fifteen minutes, not enough for a quick visit to the Sherman House—just enough for a measured stroll into work.

As you approach the gate, the barbed wire is for show; it may as well be yellow ribbons on the old oak or sparklers on a Christmas tree. I've long since lost my rookie status; the guards no longer ask to see my ID card. I know I'm here on consignment. I am without illusions: a string of numbers bracketed by a paycheck, a line in a computer program under *Inputs*.

Just inside the gate is a large sign with a simple graphic.

THIS PLANT HAS WORKED ____ ACCIDENT-FREE DAYS.

It has been reset to zero.

Sometime between yesterday and today, on a graveyard or on a dayshift, somebody crapped out.

The odds in this game were once calculated by clerks in white starched shirts with armbands, wearing crisp green visors, poring over actuarial tables. No more; now it's the quiet whir of a computer that collects the premiums deducted from each paycheck, and these are anted up and revealed in the ink of computer-generated entrails of troughs and valleys, as sharp as wolves teeth covered in red.

Somebody's been bitten.

You know, you never think it's going to happen to you. You never ever include it in any scenario—never and ever—even when the man next to you is bolted out of the blue. All you think, all you allow, is Missed Again. It's how you have to think. You can't even let yourself know you know.

Somebody got bit.

Inside the Forge is another smaller sign: This Department Has Worked ____ Accident-Free Days.

It too has been reset to zero.

Somebody I know has been bitten.

All is quiet on the western end of the Forge. I poke my head around back behind the lockers where the guys from the Merry-Go-Round hang out—nobody.

It's quiet.

Normally at the end of a shift it's quiet; almost everyone is in the change rooms. What's missing today is the knot of men—

guys who are always in early—circling around by the coffee machine.

There's some extra brass in the Forge office—not too much, nothing unusual.

I pause at centre stage, in the middle of the aisle between the office and the Six Thousand Hammer ... nothing, nothing, everything seems to be in place.

I know I'll get the news upstairs in the change room. I'm halfway through the doorway and almost onto the stairs that z-up over the crib to the change room before I see it. Out of the corner of my eye, it registers as a reflex: the Upsetter. It gets steady use but not heavy use; a fair amount of guys know how to work it. I still don't know who, but the field sure has narrowed.

The Upsetter is screened off and there is a rope barricade for order like in a bank; suspended from the rope is a STOP sign, and clipped to the sign are some papers with writing and a government logo: official forces are at work.

Someone has chalk-marked the accident site with circled foot-prints and arrows. It looks like a diagram for a football play. I try to reconcile the bright patches of blood with the cold, unflinching Upsetter. There's one thing to infer: someone's been mauled.

The change room is locked: meeting in progress. The afternoon shift supervisor comes up and posts a sign that says CLOCK ON.

Go and wait in the lunchroom; that's all he tells me.

I figure I'll go and see the blacksmith.

The blacksmith is off the beaten track; he's way down at the very far end of the Forge. He stays put for coffee and his lunch break but he's up; he's always up on the news. Smithy is like a sponge that soaks up every rumour and every nuance. And he collates it into, "Forty-one years working for the same company and I'll be getting my pension soon."

"You're looking for news I suppose, eh?" the Smithy says.

"Accidents come in threes," he says, "always in threes."

The Smithy is having his last cup of tea for the day and shuffling his gear in preparation for tomorrow. I learned a long time ago that you can't rush information out of the blacksmith; you just have to let him breeze, and if you're patient, what you want to know will come out.

"Yes, oh yes, accident number one was this morning early over in Assembly; a guy got his knee banged up pretty bad. The union's grumbling and talking grievance because the guy wasn't even supposed to be there and was only helping out of manners and following orders. And he got hurt. Then Bob from the Iron House, who knows the guy good enough to call his wife on the phone, she said how he was lucky enough to get an African doctor feller who was just coming on duty at the General. Because this African doctor fellar specializes in knees to do with football, so right away he knew what was what. Bob says that the guy from Assembly's wife told him that six weeks on crutches is what it'll take for him and then—"

"—Smithy. Who got hurt in the Forge?"

"Eh—that is accident number two."

"How did it happen?"

"Well, not long after the feller in Assembly, just before first coffee, right by the office, on the Upsetter—you know the one I mean?"

"Yes, yes. Who was working it?"

"At the time?"

"Yes!"

"Colly!"

Smithy got upset with me and fell silent. I knew if I wanted anything more out of him I had to apologize; the blacksmith could be as stubborn as an old shoe when he wanted.

"Sorry Smithy. I didn't know who—how bad? When? Just around first coffee?"

He decides to let me stew, make me sweat for it. We walk half-way back towards the lunchroom before he begins, "Yeah, Colly got hurt real bad, real bad. He lost two fingers for sure, maybe the whole hand. Plus he managed to get burns in three places— shoulder, chest, and leg.

"I didn't see so I can't say, but I heard that George the day-shift supervisor said that when he cut away Colly's pants there was a burn right up near his privates. And George says that Colly's whole cock and balls—everything—had just about disappeared up inside him.

"That happens outta fright," Smithy says. "You ever hear about that young feller?

"When I was in the war," Smithy says, "that happened to fellers all the time."

I'm thinking of Colly, late thirties and already fifteen years with the company. A drinker to be sure; the little that I know about him was mulled out over warm draft. When I first started, he was one of the fellers who showed me some shortcuts; very good mechanically, he knew how to coax that little extra out of the machines.

You have to wonder: What happens to a man like Colly now?

~

The meeting is in session.

As grim a lineup of hardened jowls as you will ever see. First up is Big Joe the General Foreman; he gives a little speech and introduces "a guy from a special team."

This guy—he's got a blackboard mounted on a tripod and a flip chart all ready to go. The suit he's wearing is a week's full piecework. He speaks of "tendencies, abuses, and accident-conducive environments." Mr. Fancy Suit recreates the accident on his blackboard. He calls it like a slow motion replay of a horse race. I can still hear the crack of excitement in his voice, blunted by the surety of the outcome: Colly reached the starting gate at 7:08 and clocked on at 7:34; before the first turn, at 9:26, he was out of the race.

Mr. Suit went on to list "contributing factors." Colly's old boots and old work clothes "may have been too comfortable," and his not wearing his face shield were all "venial sins." Colly had the furnace going "at fifty degrees over the recommended rate," and "the number of pieces completed indicates that he was working at unsafe speeds, well in excess of the piece rate for the job."

That set off a collective grumble from the change room: cough-coughing, throat-clearing, the scratch of matches, and the spark of lighters igniting cigarettes sending up fresh angry clouds of smoke as the flimsiest of veils to cover the hostility.

Mr. Suit nervously zipped through the rest of his clinic,

stopping to point a quick finger at "employee lifestyle habits." Then he cleared out along with the rest of the brass.

The Flying Hungarian, our shift foreman, walked the brass to the door and waited until they cleared the landing. Then he paced out a stretch, left to right six to eight steps, pivot, right to left, back and forth. It's a habit of his, he'd swing one hand low and the other would be cocked high as if in a sling, his chin would be just about touching his chest but his eyes would be looking up. When his pressure was up, one of the blue veins near his left temple would bulge. Today, the veins at both temples are dancing like cobras, he swivels to a stop and says: "Colly's dead."

∼

It took us a while to get started. We were running guards. Right off we had to do a reset on the hammer die. At first the die wouldn't budge. The die is held to the hammer by a pin—a metal spike—that is driven through an eye block at the top of the hammer and the die. The pin is reinforced by shims. The die is also shimmed to the gums of the hammer. A setup is never permanent, the constant relentless pounding of the hammer sees to that, hardly ever does a shift go by without a crew having to do a setup.

To knock the pin out, we have to bring in the big battering ram. The battering ram is a huge tapered club, fat and round at one end with a snub point at the other. Built right on to the hammer is a hook and chain pulley system. With the aid of the chain and pulley four men can just lever past the inertia and set the ram on a pendulum course, the rain of blows is supposed to loosen the pin enough for it to be tapped out with a sledge hammer. But not today—the pin wouldn't budge.

The crew from the Four: Zoltan, Black Charlie, Their Mike, and Small George, came over for a whack at it—no dice. Pretty soon we had a fair crowd gathered from all over the Forge, everybody wanted a crack and everybody got a crack—not a shiver.

Fat Mike goes and gets the foreman.

The Flying Hungarian rolls up his white, long-sleeved shirt, takes off his tie, and scuffs his shoes.

"Alright Mike, let's me and you show these young fuckers how to work this ram."

Black Charlie, a man not given to strenuous displays, joins them. They take a few exploratory swings. English Mike comes over. "Here," he says, "you need a man to steer."

Just about every man in the Forge is here now, crowded around the hammer. The ram is drawn back, everyone inhales: "HEAVE!" as the ram is released to ricochet off the pin, exhale: "GOOD ONE!"... "HEAVE!"

No go. Finally they stop, winded.

"Think we should get the grease gun and the compressed air? What do you think?" English Mike says.

The Flying Hungarian is bent over double trying to catch his breath; he takes a cigarette from Fat Mike and wheezes on it, "Okay, okay—one more—one more time—then we try the air."

They draw the ram back an extra step and let it rip. I can only guess what went into that blow, but I know what was behind it: over seventy years of working in the Forge. That blow rang off the pin with a different sound. Immediately, a

"HUZZA HUZZA" went up from the other side of the hammer.

That blow inspires them; they blast away at the pin and it begins to give slow, inch by torturous inch … and then all at once it comes right out.

The crowd whittles away by the twos and threes; the Flying Hungarian sticks around while we reset the die, and watches while we run a tryout. Finally, reluctantly, he turns to leave (the only time I've ever seen him walk slowly). I watch him all the way to the office: He stays in the centre of the aisle and goes right past Colly's Upsetter without stopping.

I take a long drink from the water fountain and let the water play across my face. When I close my eyes, I can still hear the ram striking the pin. I can hear the echoes of those final blows as if from far away, like church bells.

We make day-rate by ten o'clock. No one feels much like working; we troop off to the office to see if we could book an extra setup.

The Flying Hungarian is at his desk, going through an accordion stack of computer printouts.

The Flying Hungarian asks Fat Mike to see if he could find a pair of bolt cutters. And he sends me for coffee.

I get back to the office before Fat Mike. The Flying Hungarian is still staring at the stack of printouts, drumming his fingers up and down a column of figures; he motions me over and points at the printout.

> Employee No: 981
> In: 7:08
> On: 7:34
> Off: 9:26*

I hand him his coffee.

Fat Mike returns with the bolt cutters.

We go to Colly's locker.

Fat Mike snips it open on the first go.

Colly's locker is crammed with at least two dozen pairs of thongs of all shapes and sizes, two new pairs of gloves and countless old ones, a face shield, and lots of asbestos cloth. There's a shelf at eye level; up here is where Colly kept his stash of skin magazines, extra hard hats, his piecework bankbook, and in the back corner—his twenty-sixer of scotch.

The Flying Hungarian reaches in and pulls out the bottle as if it's a grenade. It's more than half-empty. He weighs it in his palm, bobbles it, and for a second I think he's going to hurl it at the wall; instead, he holds it up for Fat Mike to see his reflection. Fat Mike cringes.

There is a long minute of silence in the shadows behind the hammers.

"Get a dolly," the foreman finds his voice, "and get these thongs down to the blacksmith's shop."

Fat Mike begins to stack the thongs. I go for the dolly. When I get back, there is a small fire going in a parts bin, and Fat Mike and the Flying Hungarian are picking up as best as they can pieces of broken glass.

~

It's only 11:20 PM, but everyone is already changed and crowded around the computer terminal in front of the office. Guys coming in on graveyards are getting the news about Colly. The

Flying Hungarian has to come out and issue a statement; the events of the day are compressed into an official language: "severe trauma," "accident-induced shock," "massive renal failure," "arrangements are being made."

I punch out at 11:28. The Bayfront passes by at 11:33. If I ran I'd improve my chances, but I can't find the legs. Just as I reach the gate I see it go by; the next one's at 11:53.

Some guys are talking about going over to the Sherman House for a drink; I trail off. While I'm waiting at the bus stop, the blacksmith's voice pops into my head. I see him in a corner of my mind, pouting like a little child. I hear him saying over and over, "Accidents come in threes...."

I'm on the corner a good five minutes when the Flying Hungarian drives by; he toots me from his Buick and turns east on to Burlington Street.

I figure I've got enough time to walk west, up to the next bus stop. I'm almost there when the bus goes by, all lit up inside and empty.

ARISTOTLE LIVED ACROSS the street and up a little bit from my grandmother's house on Lewis Street. Aristotle was the eldest son of Arthur Algernon Burgess. The Headmaster. The well-known educator. A man of many letters to the editor. A virtuous, churchgoing, choir-singing man, who spoiled many a rod on the stubborn backs of us hard-headed boys in a vigorous rearguard defense of the three Rs.

As the eldest son of this man who devoted his life to the study and practice of the link between motivational fear and educational results, Aristotle was seldom seen by the rest of us. At recess Aristotle would invariably have some important errand to run on behalf of the school. As Head Boy, he took his lunch in a classroom set aside for special study. Immediately after school, Aristotle would be whisked away by Mr. Burgess in his car.

It does no justice to Mr. Burgess's prize possession to call it a car. 'Automobile' simply does not convey any of its sleek grace or powerful elegance: Mr. Burgess was the proud owner of an Opel sedan.

We had no appropriate language for the colour of Mr. Burgess's sedan: it wasn't cream, or beige, or even tan. We were at a loss to describe it. At that time, we were a nation of tea drinkers: green tea or black tea sweetened to the thickening point of syrup was the drink of choice, until coffee came into fashion with the Americans who came to install LockJoint—an island-wide sewage system that brought the first flush of prosperity. Much later, in the gush of Oil, in and among the pretensions that money buys, I learned of the perfect description for the colour of Mr. Burgess's Opel sedan; it was *café au lait*.

~

There was very little room between generations in my grandmother's house; her last child was born shortly before her first child—my mother—began having children of her own. By the time I reached secondary school, my family had exceeded the boundaries of tribe and we, like our island country, were well on our way to being a nation: an oligarchy, characterized by intense periods of immigration and rising birth rates. We were united as all nations are by the common observance of ceremony and holidays, banded by the every-day tyranny of routine. My grandmother's house was in the eye of many storms; it was our parliament, the seat of our judiciary, and a detention centre-cum-holding compound for an ever-increasing mob of children.

I was among the older children who were expected to make a meandering way back to the high court of my grandmother's house, every day after school. This twenty-minute walk took at least a zigzagging hour. There were several rendezvous points where cousins and siblings from different schools would meet up to synchronize alibis and excuses, to form a loose procession that closed ranks as we neared Lewis Street.

Aristotle would, of course, already be at home by the time I neared my grandmother's house. He would be at work washing his father's sedan. Mr. Burgess insisted upon his sedan being thoroughly washed the moment it arrived home, after a drive of any duration or distance, no matter the inclemency of the weather. This suited Aristotle particularly well; washing the sedan was his daily dose of freedom. Like so many of the modest houses along the street, the Burgess household had no garage. The bit of driveway that could have served instead had been turned into a living-room adjunct for the burgeoning Burgesses. The Opel was always and perforce parked on the street. Aristotle made good advantage of this circumstance; he would inch his way down to the corner, where his view of the important intersection of Independence Avenue was unimpeded. Aristotle could listen to the frenzied practicing of the Mad Hatters Steel Orchestra while keeping his eyeballs peeled on the parade of Catholic and Presbyterian schoolgirls who adventured along the avenue.

One of my favourite stopping places on the way home from school was at the workshop of a carpenter who was totally blind and made only Morris chairs. I would try my best to sneak up on the carpenter and filch a few scraps of wood to practice my karate chops. The carpenter would always catch me out and sneer at me for being "such a clumsy oaf that even a blind man can see you coming from a mile."

On his boldest days, Aristotle would cross the street and come over to greet me at the carpenter's workshop. He tried to rid himself of his father's shadow by swearing and being as crude as he knew how to be. He was always eager to talk; his favorite subject was girls.

Aristotle had discovered girls the way Columbus discovered

the West Indies—with a great deal of excitement, and like Columbus—he was also totally off base.

"Did you see how that Convent girl was smiling up at me?" Aristotle could turn even the smallest hint into a huge encouragement. "If a Catholic girl say that she like you, you're bound to get a fock. They have a religious obligation to go forth and multiply. But she have to say it out loud or it won't count."

"You ready for the A-Levels?" Aristotle's other obsession was school. He was already cramming for exams that were two years away. He could recite a list of every available scholarship and the grade requirements for each.

The carpenter was well aware of the short leash that Aristotle was attached to and teased him mercilessly.

"I don't want you standing around my shop too long," the carpenter would say to Aristotle. "You might learn something your daddy don't want you to learn. You might learn a trade. Your daddy will give me a taste of his strap if I learn you a trade. You better hurry up and go home to your school books. You done black already; mind your studies, or your daddy will beat you blue!"

Aristotle never had a rebuttal that could counter the truth of the carpenter's words. And while his eyes roamed over the approach and especially the depart of every passing girl, his sight never strayed too far away from the Opel. At the first glimpse of any shadow such as a younger sibling or—god forbid—the looming hulk of his father, Aristotle would dart back across the street.

The washing of the Opel was a precise drill to be performed in an exacting series of steps. The initial rinse was done with a bucket of clean water. All of the floor mats and all four hubcaps were removed and put to soak before the second stage: a thorough soaping of the body and wheel wells. The second rinse was accomplished with a fine spray from a garden hose. The Opel was then patted—not wiped—dry, in readiness for a coat of wax. After the wax, a clear polish was applied, for buffing only. Then, two coats of a special polish, "to achieve a deeper, longer-lasting shine." The last step, after the floor mats and hubcaps were put back on, was to start the sedan and move it forward about six inches to a foot, so that portion of the tires that was resting on the road could also receive a cleaning.

On his sixteenth birthday, Aristotle was given the privilege of starting the Opel and inching it forward. On many of those after-school afternoons, by the time I passed by Mr. Burgess's house, his Opel would be sparkling clean and Aristotle would still be sitting inside, behind the wheel, transported. In all my life so far, Aristotle is the only person that I know of who was granted permission, who had a license to imagine.

∼

The ostensible reason for marching to my grandmother's house after school was to bivouac and wait for my father to come and pick us up when he finished work. The real reason was so that my mother could continue to hold her position in the ruling junta.

In the nation of my family, the line between junta and cabal was criss-crossed so often that it had all but disappeared. The ruling junta consisted of my mother and any three of her siblings. The cabal was comprised of those out of favour who hatched coup and counter-coup while awaiting their return to the inner circle.

New nations have a tendency to be founded on or to succumb to personality cults; they quickly become one-party states where Prime Ministers promote themselves to Presidents and are then outmaneuvered by the impatient next generation into constitutionally important but nearly powerless figureheads. My grandmother held the largely ceremonial post of Governor General.

The second storey of my grandmother's house doubled as a public gallery where, between four and six o'clock, from teatime to supper-time, on every weekday, court was in session. The docket was always full; justice was swift and absolute. The wisdom of Solomon gave way to the pragmatism of Alexander the Great. Decisions cut straight through to the quick: if whatever was in dispute could not somehow be equally shared, then it was taken away from all.

The only power that my grandmother wielded at these weekday proceedings was that of moral suasion. Occasionally she would cite precedent from her vast store of common law and influence the outcome of a case. Yet my grandmother had an important and essential role: you could appeal to her and receive a sympathetic hearing, although no verdict, once made, was ever overturned. On the weekend, however, things were quite different.

On Saturdays my grandmother had absolute power over the mob of children who were left in her care. My grandmother was a Saturday Czarina. She ruled, she inspired terror, with two simple implements of torture: a teacup and a tablespoon.

My grandmother was a person who enjoyed indisputable good health, which she attributed to her regime of folk remedies and home-brewed medicines. At the first sign of a "fresh cold," my grandmother would douse herself in a concoction of coconut oil and Vicks VapoRub. Aches and pains were soothed away with a black tar-like substance made in Guyana but known as *Canadian Healing Oil.* The first principle in my grandmother's homeopathic schema was KYBO. Keep Your Bowels Open.

"Saturday morning first thing," she designated as the right time for "a flushing and a cleansing." All of her grandchildren, without exception, had to line up to be given one tablespoon of cod liver oil and one teacup full of senna tea. The senna tea was sweetened with honey to help chase down the taste of the cod liver oil. A well-steeped cup of senna is a most powerful laxative, but when taken in conjunction with cod liver oil it has military implications. The Geneva Convention against the cruel treatment of prisoners of war should have been invoked on my grandmother.

In our new nation, pounds, shillings, and pence were giving way to dollars and cents, but some Imperial measures remained: on a typical Saturday there would be at least a dozen and quite often more than a score of us under the roof of my grandmother's house. For the next several hours, none of us could dare to stray more than a few feet away from the one and only toilet. By Saturday afternoon, a somewhat flushed bunch of children were more than willing to give their grandmother the space she demanded when watching her favourite TV show, *Wrestling From Chicago.*

"Oh Geed! Oh Geed! Oh Geed!"

My grandmother would shout at the behemoths on the TV screen. "Hit him one for me. Oh Geed! Oh Geed!"

My grandmother said "Oh Geed" because it was a sin to take the name of the Lord thy God in vain.

Ray "Golden" Apollon was by far her favourite wrestler. He was a native son who had gone out into the wide world and made it big.

Big was the operative word when talking about Ray "Golden" Apollon. He was a big man, with a thick mane of hair, and as advertised in his press release, "with the chiseled torso and strength of a Greek god."

Apollon entered into my grandmother's living room and her fantasies for a few seasons via the magic of television. At various times he was The Undisputed, The National, The International, The Far Eastern, The Afro-Caribbean, The Champion of the World and the Known Universe. He was a professional wrestler. He was on the circuit that emanated out of Chicago; he always played The Good Guy.

This endeared him to my grandmother all the more. Good and Evil were the corner-posts in the ring of her life. And like Ray "Golden" Apollon, she too fought the good fight.

Apollon returned home to Trinidad periodically from his world travels, in his off-season. Sometimes, to keep himself in shape and cash, he would try and stir up a little local interest. Apollon was media wise, he knew how to give and get good copy. He made it a business priority to pose for the local press in the skimpy regalia of his trade. On one such occasion, he showed off his World Heavyweight Championship Belt.

New nations are starved for heroes: achieve something today and your face will be on a stamp tomorrow. It was swiftly decided to give Ray "Golden" Apollon, World Champion, a parade.

The parade was set to run right down Independence Avenue. The Devil and his dogs could not keep my grandmother away.

Early on the Saturday morning of the parade, there were a lot of eager volunteers willing to escape the teacup and spoon to go and stake out a prime spot for her. I won the job.

LockJoint had finally reached my grandmother's street. The Americans had the latest in technology and the most advanced systems for project management. They had something called "just in time delivery." We had "just now" time. The whole street was dug up, on both sides, except for a narrow strip down the middle barely wide enough to walk on. A car needed at the least three people to get through a street that LockJoint was working on: one to steer and two to push.

Mr. Burgess was like a king without a country; for months, he had nowhere to park his Opel. He had tried parking a few blocks away from his home, but his distinctive sedan was too tempting a target and had already suffered from an act of vandalism. The suspects were many, anyone from a legion of past or present students who had felt the sting of his strap. Mr. Burgess had no choice but to call upon the police and ask them to keep his Opel safe in their impound. This provoked a lot of gossip. It was such a shame how the Headmaster couldn't keep up with his hire purchase payments; the police had to seize his nice car.

Aristotle gained the most from the breakdown in the

Burgess family routine. He joined the entourage that made its meandering way to Louis Street. Aristotle had a new passion— music. It made him bold and desperate enough to dare to openly challenge his father's strap. More than once he had been seen making music in the pan yard of the Mad Hatters Steel Orchestra.

On the morning of the parade for Apollon, Aristotle joined me and we picked our way over the rubble of the street, down to the corner where The Mad Hatters were tuning up their steel pans in readiness for the parade.

"Both of you still in short pants and you want to talk about playing pan?" The blind carpenter put the finishing touches on another Morris chair while we made the small talk of boys trying to sound like men.

We crossed over to Independence Avenue. Corn was in season and under the eaves of the corner shop, street vendors were already set up for the day. The coal pot smells of *boil corn* and *roast corn* were in sweet competition. Aristotle and I gained the front lines and as the parade approached in the pushing and shoving, the craning and straining to see this freshly minted hero, I heard my grandmother's voice shouting, "Make way! Oh Geed! Let me pass!"

Independence Avenue went from low tide to high sea: There was something in the rising tide of nationalism, something that I have come to recognize as its undertow. Apollon was proof, like some latter-day Columbus, that *yes* it was possible to dare and go beyond the unknown edge. But what was being celebrated? His return? Or the fact that it could be done?

Aristotle would make his way out, not from the book-learning that his father relentlessly tried to beat into him, but through music, by the beating of notes onto an oil drum, as a member of the Mad Hatters Steel Orchestra.

In the nation of my family, we had to learn how to make the subtractions for death, our birth rate slowed, and emigration exceeded immigration for the first time. I was among the first wave of émigrés. I cannot say exactly when it ceased to be, but my grandmother's house is no longer the centre of the universe.

"N-O IS NO. You can't understand? Or what? Read my lips: N-O is NO.

"Did you understand that? Now march your tail and pack. And don't let me have to tell you again. No!"

"Why?" He pleads again for the thousandth time. "But why why why, Mom? Why-I-have-to-go-Tunapuna?" He insists until his voice peaks and breaks up into a falsetto crackle.

"Look here…" she out-stares him, "don't get me vex. March inside and pack your things, you hear?"

"But why-do-I-have-to-go? Mom?" He stomps in a slow funeral refrain from the kitchen to his bedroom.

"Now look, you making me vex, boy, I'm warning you, don't try my patience."

"But why?" he whinnies, a gangling colt refusing to leave the barn.

His mother gathers her breath and snorts her reply.

"Young man, don't play you hard-headed with me. Did you pack your toothbrush? And pajamas? You have enough Jockey shorts for the week? Look sharp, look here. I'm giving you five dollars. Five ones. Put one in each pocket, so if you lose one you won't lose all. Remember to share with your cousins. Don't buy *anchar* and *barrah* from people selling by the side of the road. If you go cinema, don't go in Pit; you pay the extra and go in House. Listen to what your auntie say; if I find out you give her any trouble I will cut your tail, not once, but twice. Play nice with your cousins. You bigger than them; you must let them win sometimes for manners. And speaking of manners, I don't want you going quite Tunapuna to shame me in front of your auntie. Keep your elbows off the table. Use a knife, not your fingers. Don't wolf down your food. Take your time and chew. When you finish eat, ask permission first, before you leave the table. Look here, take this. This is extra money for the taxi.

"Is best to catch a new taxi. Try and get a window seat, is a long, long, hot drive. Make sure and ask the driver to show you where to change taxis in Port of Spain. Tell him you going Tunapuna via the Eastern Main Road. Your daddy and me will come up early Sunday morning for you. We go make a day of it, at Maracas beach. Maracas or Las Cuevas. Come come. You ready yet? You getting too big you know. Look how I have to tiptoe to give you a kiss."

～

Sky so clear and blue. But he is under a cloud.

Now how she expect me to jump the ravine with this suitcase in my hand? Now I can't even take the shortcut. Now I must walk all the way around. Now why I must go Tunapuna? For four whole days. Look-July done halfway finish already. Next thing you know is my holidays gone—whoosh, and is back I back in school again. Fock!

He tries the word out aloud again, still pleased with its nasal power to excite, as good as a really good hack and spit; he marks time with it until it loses its power to the roar of traffic on

Point-a-Pierre road. He has to dodge in and out of the bleat and snarl of angry snails, twisted halfway out of their shells angling for a better view, stuck in the current transmitted by pedestrian relay to roadside vendors, carrying the news of a big big and getting bigger with each telling, accident.

By the time he reaches the scene where coarse diamonds from smashed windshields are scattered everywhere like buckshot, two policemen are marking and measuring the rubber and blood skid-marks, and a swarm of eyewitnesses buzz about a squad car where a third policeman is writing down the particulars. A superheated argument between two factions of witnesses is about to boil over. He has to slow his march to allow for the crowd, and to confirm the impression that speed makes when translated by impact into violence.

The crowd feeds on this toxic gasoline mixture of fascination and revulsion and on itself: Who? Who? cries from its fringe echo back with telegraph speed to its epicenter. Death! gets announced and confirmed in the same gulping exclamation. One bystander relates to another's near escape; strangers find common comfort in other accidents recalled and reprised, matching scars in the show-me-yours-I'll-show-you-mine way of patients. Using his suitcase and all of his fourteen years as a shield, he breaks an exit through these cobwebs; nothing clings to him, no threads of acceptance, no denial. Death has no claim on him. It is as far as, or preposterously further away than, the moon, where right now, if you could believe it, the Yankee and them say they heading there, full speed, to land a man.

∽

"Tall boy! Tall boy! Come go."

One overeager taxi driver has wrestled his suitcase away and is about to stash it in the trunk of his car.

"Tall boy," another driver tries a different tactic. "Look, I have an 8-Track with the latest sounds. You really want to drive so far with just his big mouth and Radio Trinidad for company?"

A third driver sidles into the fray with an even more compelling argument; "Psst! Smart boy, look for yourself and see if I done eh have four passengers already. You go make it five. Look them only have two and three each. Five is a trip. Come with me and is roll we ready to roll."

This argument wins out. Now his trip is real, and now he can't hide his excitement under teenage indifference. This will be the absolute furthest he's ever been allowed to venture by himself. He claims his window seat and has an uneasy moment of panic, until he pats down all of his pockets to make sure that his fortune is still intact.

The big accident on Point-a-Pierre Road forces the driver to go around the San Fernando hill, up Coffee Street onto Circular Road and then down St. Joseph's Road to the bypass. It also provides the topic of conversation until they clear Marabella.

After Marabella, the road climbs to greet the Texaco refinery on the high wide side of a hill, before snaking down through waving cane fields to hug the shoreline, roughly parallel, until Couva.

The long-run taxi driver must master a special etiquette if he is to be a success. He must engage all of his passengers, equally somehow, taking care that those who love to talk get a hearing, and for those who like to listen, something worthwhile to hear.

He has to direct the pace of the conversation with a skill at least equal to his mastery of the road, sensing when a subject is about to be exhausted or changing gears from angel to devil's advocate. Before you leave his taxi, he must have you so sold that you will make a point of looking for him when next you travel.

This particular driver is a king of the road, with years of long-run experience; this trip, he calculates, will be a tough one. A funny group: the tall boy in the back seat sticking close to the window; a fat lady with powder caked into her mustache, spread out next to the boy; and a quiet, quiet Indian man, thin like a cutlass. In the front seat, Mr. Bramble, one of his regular customers, a retired County Council man, who always claims asthma and control of the window seat. Which is fine; how he could mind when a prime brown-skin girl, no more than sixteen is his bet, ends up seated in the middle next to him— except she's wearing a white dress with plenty starch, and starch does make him scratch.

He tries to open with upcoming election talks, but no nibbles, not even from Bramble, who on another trip claimed he used to drink with Weeks—the big union man, who is in the running. One peep in the rearview mirror and the look on the fat lady's face tells him religion is out. Sports is a miss, with cricket out of season and football just starting. He would love to bring sex into the chat and see what the brown-skin girl have to say, but experience has taught him not to start off with sex. Sex is the kind of topic you have to slip in when the talk already going sweet; you have to bring it in as an example, then if it springs some roots, let it bloom on its own.

Just as he starts to despair, Bramble comes up with a subject that breaks the ice. "You think the Yankee and them could really reach and put a man way up on the moon?"

"But how you mean?" the brown-skin girl seated next to Bramble answers. "You eh see them making preparations on the television?"

The fat lady in the back seat sucks her teeth and holds a thin note, like air being pinched from a balloon. "The television is only make-believe."

The boy pauses, hearing his mother's often repeated sermon on talking to strangers and cutting in on big people's conversation ringing in his ears, but he decides to jump in: "What about Panorama News, Sports with Raffy Knowles, and the Daily Weather? All that eh real?"

The driver laughs and checks the rearview mirror, "The sharp boy have a point."

The fat lady spreads herself out a bit more, "That eh what I mean at all. Television is make-believe. How is we to know for a surety if they really reach the moon? Is only the Yankee saying so for so. Them still vex the Russian and them beat them hands down by going up into Outer Space first."

The thin Indian fella nods alliance with her. "I done see plenty matinee, plenty, where them Yankee done reach even Mars."

"Matinee is different," the driver qualifies. "Cinema is pure make-believe. And only make-believe; that is truth."

The fat lady bristles, setting waves of flesh in motion. "The television is cinema too. I have a sister in the States, last year she come down for a visit, eh-eh, see if she eh know all the episodes off by heart. She could tell me endings for weeks ahead. She say the shows we get down here done stale up there already."

"That is truth," the driver agrees, "but the news is the news."

The fat lady sucks her teeth, "Take Panorama News. It does come on at seven o'clock, every evening prompt, right? Then once the intro music done, a local announcer does come on and say in a highfalutin' voice, 'And now for the news of today.' What is the next thing that does happen?"

After a five-second lapse, the boy volunteers brightly, "A commercial?" The fat lady glares at him, but the other passengers cackle.

"No," she is serious serious, "they does show a clip of film from somewhere. That film done shoot, right?" She lets that notion settle. "The Yankee and them don't like to lose, when them see the Russians outsmarting them, they vex. Mr. President run and pick up the phone and call up Hollywood. Next thing you know is Man Landing On The Moon, showing on the television, and every man Jack believe is bound to be true."

The fat lady leans back and gives her face a quick mopping, soaking up some of the powder.

Bramble finally rebuts, "Is crow the Yankee and them love to crow, is true. But that is why self I feel them not lying. Them Yankee really know how to put a man up on the moon. And that is why self we hearing them bragging and showing off for so."

The other passengers nod consensus on this view, except for the fat lady, but she has made her point and earned respect. The driver revises his thinking; this run is turning out nice nice after all, and look, here's Couva coming up already. Experience tells him the conversation has momentum enough of its own; now is the time for him to start inserting questions, to try for some return business.

"Tall boy, you sure is quite Tunapuna you want to go?" The driver straightens the rosary beads tangled around his rearview mirror.

"Is quite Tunapuna you going? All by yourself." The brown-skin girl leans back to smile at him, "You sure you not going to go and get lost now?"

"I've been to Tunapuna before," he replies, trying to sound casual. "But never by taxi alone." He can't hide his interest or his nervousness.

"I'm going Barataria," she says, "I can show you how to get to Tunapuna. We can catch the same taxi in Port of Spain."

The driver has a good view of her legs, the way her white dress is hiked up as she keeps the upper half of her torso turned to tease and flirt with the boy in the back seat. The driver sighs, and steers the conversation onto a favorite topic of his: infamous murder cases; "Bramble, you remember the Head in the Flowerpot?"

"Yes yes, a big big case, yes man," Bramble comes back from his daydream, "They never yet find the body. Not so?"

"Is so," the driver laughs. "Tall boy, maybe you could help them out, when you reach Tunapuna."

After Couva the road opens up and the mountains of the northern range appear, as sudden and as sunny as the brown-skin girl's gat-tooth smile growing wider, coming closer to Port of Spain.

~

"Boy, I was just getting ready to send out a search party for you.

What happen? You stop to lime in Port of Spain. Come and let me give you a hug and a kiss. Or you think you getting too big for that? Let me look at you. You getting too big in truth; soon I'm going to have to jump up and kiss you. You looking more and more like your daddy. You must be thirsty and tired? Come and drink some cold juice."

For once he was glad that his aunt could carry on a complete conversation, supplying both questions and answers by herself. No, he wasn't tired, or thirsty, just strangely lightheaded; in fact, he could still hear Kamala—the girl from the taxi—singing, insisting, "You have to come Barataria and see me, before you go back San Fernando." His aunt is busily plotting and planning activities for his stay; all there is for him to do is to nod, grin, and let his imagination return to speculating on what was under that white dress. He can still smell her perfume.

"Wait until you meet Roach," his aunt says. "You and him have the same age. He lives by his granny, the neighbour next door. He's a real country bookie, with good good old-fashioned manners. You could do something for me now? You could run down to the corner shop and pick up a few things? I bet you go see Roach there, liming outside the shop, he and some other boys. I don't know what the attraction is."

~

The shop on the corner of Jubilee Street and the Tunapuna main road is little more than a parlour with an ice cooler. His aunt was right; there is a spill of teenage boys in and around the shop. One boy separates from the clutch and approaches him.

"You the neighbour family from San Fernando?" the boy asks in a serious but polite voice. "I is Roach.

"You have a five cents?" Roach asks in the same grave manner.

"Man, I don't meet you five seconds yet, and you done asking for a five cents?"

"You have a five cents," Roach insists. "Give me a five cents and I go show you something I bet you don't see everyday in San Fernando."

He hands a coin over to Roach, warily.

Roach calls over one of the younger boys. "Batman, go in the shop and buy five cents ice, and bring it back to me."

"Stay here, right here," Roach instructs him. The other boys gather around. After a minute, he finds out what the attraction at the shop is: the twin features on the girl behind the counter.

She is expertly unaware of the commotion she causes when bending; the dress she wears is loose and she performs without the restraining benefit of a bra. Whenever a customer enters, the boys cluster to the Jubilee Street side of the shop, hoping for a block of ice to be among the purchases. The best and most tantalizing viewing time is now, late in the afternoon with sunlight streaming into the shop, when she has to dig down deep into the cooler. As she jiggles the block of ice free, the knot of boys tightens and reels collectively forward. She always leaves her audience dangling.

Batman brings the ice back to Roach, who deftly wraps it in the tail of his shirt and takes a few practice karate chops at the ice block before smashing it against a concrete standpipe. The boys line up for the ice. Roach offers him first choice, then distributes the rest.

He scans from Roach's serious face to the others, joining in the loose circle of boys in kaleidoscope motion, bare feet playing like piano keys on hot asphalt, sucking and sighing on pieces of ice under the hot afternoon sun.

"Look," he smiles and produces, "a five cents."

~

After dinner, he is left to babysit. His aunt and uncle are the excited guests of a neighbour in the next block "who have a brand-new Sylvania television set. After all, is history in the making, is man landing on the moon, tonight."

He and Roach are staked out under a lamppost across the street, where they can keep an eye on the house and the steady procession of Seventh-day Adventists marching off to a Revival meet.

Roach points at the moon with a stick. "You think the Yankee and them could really reach as far up as the moon?" Roach says, unconvinced.

"Roach, you sound just like a big fat woman in the taxi coming up today. She refuse to believe. She say is only Hollywood make-believe."

"Like a Western, or a Kickup?" Roach sees the possibility right away.

"A kickup? What's a kickup, Roach?"

"Man, you know—a Kung Fu or a Karate movie."

"Roach, is everybody in Tunapuna does talk funny or just you?"

"The word eh reach San Fernando yet, that is all," Roach rebuts.

"Hah! Don't make me laugh. San Fernando is New York if you talking Tunapuna."

"Is so?" Roach gets competitive. "How much cinema San Fernando have? We have two right here in Tunapuna, and two more right in Curepe, but the one in Curepe does show only Indian pictures."

"Roach, Roach," he shakes his head, "in San Fernando it have nine—ten, it even have a drive-in."

Roach falls silent, impressed. "How far to San Fernando?"

"I had was to take two long-run taxis. Is forty-something miles to Port of Spain, and then another fifteen maybe twenty to out here. Sixty miles, easy. At least."

Roach is even more impressed, and excited. "You bound to drive pass the sea, coming up, right?"

"Yeah, some of the time, a good bit."

"What's it like?" Roach says in his serious, curious way.

"Is a long, long drive man. Two hours almost to Port of Spain, and then another one and change to out here. But I stopped in Barataria and changed taxis."

"No, I mean what's it like—the sea?"

"Roach! You mean to tell me you never yet see the sea?"

"Yes. No I never yet."

"You lie. Roach, you lie. Don't lie to me Roach. Is true? You never yet see the sea. Is true?"

"Yes man, is true," Roach says, embarrassed now. "We from the country. I only just move down here by my granny when my mammy gone. She gone Port of Spain, or could even be as far as San Fernando," Roach shrugs. "My granny say—she gone to hell."

Roach hunches his shoulders and rocks silently on the balls of his feet, nodding to the last of the Seventh-day Adventists as they hurry past, backs stiff, heads bowed, to the Revival.

Silence joins them on the curb. He pulls the stick away from Roach, trying to shoo it away before it gets too settled. He looks hopefully back to the moon for a change of subject. "The moon eh really Up, you know. It's Out. It out in Outer Space."

Roach continues to bob on the balls of his feet, his arms stretched out in front of him for balance. He is looking up too, but only as far as the lamppost where generations of insects are trapped in the halo of the streetlight, circling, wings beating in tight, frantic orbits decaying into the light.

He traces with the stick for Roach, in loose gravel, patterns of famous battles fought in History—recounts the devious plots from movies he has seen until a clear channel reopens. Roach is an expert on Westerns; they work and revise scene by scene, role by role, through Roach's current favourites, The Magnificent Seven and High Noon.

And up above—or is it out—the moon climbs across the night, clinging close to the sky and the very last of its innocence.

~

"What it have to do here in Tunapuna on a Saturday afternoon, Roach?"

Roach is more solemn than usual. "I have to go Revival."

"Come on, come and go cinema. I have money; don't worry with that. Come go nah Roach."

But Roach won't budge. "I have to go Revival." Roach is

under direct orders and the very real threat of pain from his granny. Not even the enticement of a free cinema show can lure him; Roach's granny has a heavy hand. Today is the last day of the Seventh-day Adventists' Revival meet, and it is the Sabbath; Roach knows, he knows he has to go.

"Why you don't come to the Revival?" Roach says.

"Who me? You mad or what, I is a Catholic. They won't allow me inside."

"How they could know if you is a Catholic? It write anywhere on your forehead? I don't see it. What happen? You 'fraid?"

"No. I eh 'fraid."

"Well come go," Roach presses him.

"One church is plenty enough for me."

"Man you 'fraid. Admit it," Roach trumps.

"No way! Not me. I ready if you ready. Come go." He follows suit.

~

The church can't hide the fact that it too is a convert, from a one-time warehouse to a sometimes community centre; the steps have a new railing and the double doors rounded at the top are several collections away from being painted. Inside, folding chairs are queued into tight rows, and a few cushions are scattered among the elderly and the infirm. The devout have all hemmed in near the front, where the preacher is prowling on a raised 4' x 4' dais.

"Welcome Brother! Welcome Sister!" he booms over the

hymn, announcing each newcomer to the swiveling stares of his congregation. "Welcome Two Young Brothers!"

Roach slides into a seat near the back, keeping his head bowed all the while. He follows, sticking close to Roach. At his first quick glance it doesn't look much like a church to him at all, and it seems as if the preacher was just waiting for them, because as soon as they reach their seats he waves a signal to shut the double doors. But once the doors are closed it becomes unmistakably a church. Pins of light stitch around the windows, weaving ornate patterns of twilled gold among the dust motes, and the hard black of the preacher's cloth becomes subtle with purple. The preacher's voice soars, now free from hymn, with the rasp of the American South in his gospel, and the ring of redemption in each step across the 4' x 4' stage.

When the preacher leans against his dais, gulping air in great lungfuls, oiling the shine of his sweat onto his sleeve, then the first collection hymn starts and the plates are passed—and Roach besides him lifts his grave voice up, joining in rapture as the hymn gathers the congregation together in faith. He hears a low, growling, hesitant sound and locates it as coming from his throat, the inarticulate speech of his heart. The rattle of the collection plate adds to his constriction; in a rising panic, he turns away from Roach and slides and stumbles away out of the Revival.

~

"You sure is just cinema you going? Smelling so sweet." His aunt is wise to him. "Well Mister man, don't forget where you living. Don't you be coming home too late."

He struts down Jubilee Street puffed up with gunslinger courage that deflates as soon as he boards the taxi on the main road. Can he even find back her house? What to talk to her about? He can afford tickets for the cinema, but what about eats after? The taxi speeds along; every bump it hits is another question on the road to Barataria. But he can see the space between her teeth in her smile, and the heave of her white dress is memory enough to keep him going.

~

"Boy! You mean to say you didn't see them land?" She says it overloud, as if scandalized. "Remember that fat lady in the taxi day before? You know, she could very well be right," she nods and checks off her criticisms on her fingers. "The reception was poor throughout; too much snow and ghosts on the screen; you couldn't tell what from what. And the sound was scratchy scratchy—"

"Kamala!" A youngster comes racing out to the gallery. "Mammy say you must come in the kitchen and bring some cold juice for your friend from San Fernando."

"What you doing quite here in Barataria?" The youngster asks in wily innocence his mother's muttered question. His embarrassed sister chases him inside; pleased that he's some-how done his best to annoy her, he returns to his place, inches from the television set. Four generations of her family are grouped around the set, along with neighbours and invited guests. One very old woman is wrapped up tight in a sari and seated in the place of honour, from her Morris chair, she directs a loud monologue in Hindi at the set. No one seems to mind.

He is left to feel foolish for coming all this way and alone in the darkness of the gallery, as she is seconded into serving refreshments and readying her younger sisters for bed. When she returns, it is to enlist his help in steering elderly neighbours down the steep front steps. Her main chore is to initiate the novices among the neighbours and relatives into the magic of television. As each new show comes on, she is called upon for detailed plot summaries and in-depth biographies of the leading characters. His idea of going to the cinema is abandoned for an episode of Bonanza. She doesn't like to miss Little Joe. When a large, satisfied group of neighbours leave all at once, he goes from standing out in the gallery to sinking into a sofa in the living room. Finally, all her chores attended to, she smiles her gat-tooth smile and snuggles in beside him as the detective action of Mannix unfolds.

They settle down and watch until the national anthem. After sign-off, she leads him back out to the gallery. As the last of the neighbours leave, they take turns teasing her and "her San Fernando boyfriend." She sits, her smile very close to him. Her mother finds reasons to flit in and out, finally calling her daughter into the kitchen.

She comes back pouting; he is already standing in some confusion at the head of the steps. "You best go now," she leads him down the stairs. "You go have a hard enough time trying to catch a taxi back to Tunapuna at this hour of the night."

She unlatches the gate; he drags his feet and looks at the moon. "So ... it have a man in the moon now, for truth."

She smiles. He feels his heartbeat race and again a rising constriction in his throat. She leads him behind the thick shelter of a hibiscus hedge, then on tiptoe, she adds the quick surprise of her tongue to his, letting him press against her and feel for hidden treasure.

"You better get going," she pushes him away.

"I—I'll—"

She steals his breath with another kiss, eludes the tangle of his hands again, and smiling, skips away behind the hibiscus.

He can feel his palm tingle, remembering where it touched her warm flesh, and see the width of her retreating smile in the headlights of the taxi, all the way back to Jubilee Street.

~

"Where is he? Where is that boy? Girl, if you could have seen the horrors he gave me to get him out of the house and come up here. Now is time to go and you think I could find him?"

His aunt laughs with his mom, "That is always the way. I bet you he with Roach, liming down by the corner. I'm surprised he didn't see you drive up. Just let me turn off this pot. And take a look outside. What I tell you, look he and Roach coming now."

"He didn't give you any trouble?" his mother asks.

"Not at all, child, none at all. He and Roach hit it off. I think he even pick up a girlfriend somewhere. Last night he said he going cinema but he was smelling too sweet."

"A girlfriend?" his mother exclaims. "Girl, you sure? I don't think I ready for that yet. They does get big so quick."

"I know, I know," his aunt agrees, "I was so surprised when

I saw him this time, after only a few months. I can just imagine how tall he's going to end up."

"Girl," his mother sighs, "he just shoot up like a beanstalk, after Carnival. When he was small I used to tease him by telling him how one day he go be able to drink soup off my head, now is true." They laugh.

He and Roach stop to finish off their ice at the lamppost across the street. Roach stoops and admires, "PL license, that is a new Ford all-yuh have, man."

"Yeah," he grins. "Do you know what my dad says Ford stands for? Fix Or Repair Daily."

"What happen?" his mother calls out, "You forget me already? Come for a hug and a kiss, or you think you is too much man for that now? I hear you have a girlfriend now? Is so?"

"Mom!" He looks at his aunt in exasperation.

"You ready to go Maracas? Go and get your things. Ask your father for the key and put them in the trunk."

"Mom? Can Roach come with us? To Maracas."

"No, I don't think so. The car full-up already with us, your uncle and auntie, and your cousins."

"Roach never yet see the sea."

He, his mother, and his aunt look over at Roach bobbing on the balls of his feet over by the lamppost.

"You done invite him already?" his aunt asks.

"No," he says.

"The car is full," his mother says with finality.

"Man done land on the moon and Roach never yet even see the sea," he looks at his mom. "Take Roach to Maracas instead of me. I've been there already, please. Please Mom."

His mom thinks about it, "There's only one thing to do," she says. "Go and ask your father."

~

There are two ways to get to Maracas; the better road is the one from Port of Spain up through Maraval and then over the Northern Range. They opt for the other way, which is much closer from Tunapuna, through Curepe to St. Joseph winding up into the mountains, but the drive is pure torture.

"Oh God, Roach. You is only bone, boy, like a fish," he yelps, after the car hits yet another pothole. Roach is sitting on his lap, twisting and turning eager every which way to get a better view out the window.

"Roach it eh have nothing to see but cocoa and coffee until we reach the Junction, so take it easy and breathe light," he pleads.

But Roach can hardly contain his excitement, "How far we reach? How much more road to cover?"

He can see even less than Roach, but feels the car climbing and is glad when his dad announces the Junction.

Roach becomes fascinated by the way in which plants grow out of the side of the mountains. "Look, balisea. Snake does hide in balisea."

His father laughs, "Careful what you say, Roach; that is the PNM Party flower."

"But is true, Mister is true," Roach is glad to dispense some country wisdom. "Snake does hide in balisea and bird pepper tree."

They begin the steep descent into Maracas. Roach strains but it's hard for him to see around sharp curves, and the patches of blue horizon flash by too quickly through vs in the trees and remain unfocused in his imagination.

"What is that? What is that I hearing?" Roach asks, excited. No one has to answer him. "I hear it." His voice breaks, "I hear it roar."

Then, as they round a final curve and come into sudden panoramic focus, Roach intakes sharply and goes rigid.

"Roach, Oh God Roach," he croaks from where he is wedged into the seat. "Boy, you better start back breathing."

They tumble out of the car and race to the sea.

Roach is in the lead, but he slows in the thick surprise of hot sand and comes to a complete stop, shy, at the water's edge.

He runs past Roach, high-kicking over the breaking waves, turning to splash and yell, "Come on, come on in." He waves at Roach, in big xs from beyond the breakers.

Roach spreads his arms out as far as he can, as if trying to measure the sweep of the ocean. His eyes swivel away from the sun to the bend of the horizon where a pale moon is making its diminishing way into history. Roach sustains a revving note from deep in his belly. He taxies through the waves into the sea.

EACH ONE TEACH ONE

IN THE WEEKS before her first trip overseas, Cornelia was flooded with good but often conflicting pieces of advice by her friends and fellow workers at the church. 'Take everything you need with you.' 'Less is best'. 'Good connections are the best surprise.' 'Expect the unexpected.' 'Traveling is more of an innate art than a learned science.' 'The hardest thing to carry is conviction.' Cornelia thoroughly enjoyed every minute of the sweet agony of sorting through all of this collective wisdom; she was bound for Guyana and determined to 'be a participant, not a passenger' on the trip of her lifetime.

Cornelia Alexandria Bretton narrowly missed out—by a stroke and a heart attack—on becoming Mrs. Horace Michael Walters. If poor Horace had only listened to his heart, who knows? But Horace was a man who seldom listened. Cornelia was a bookworm of twenty-two, Catholic, and overwhelmed. Horace was well into his forties with (as it turned out) every right to be worried about his fifties. He was also a Catholic, separated but not divorced. Nowadays it is next to impossible to meet anyone over thirty who has not spent some time in that particular limbo, but when Horace died, leaving all of his business unfinished, Cornelia discovered that she could not even claim common-law status for herself, and that the sympathy and consolation of her church was also the property of Horace's widow.

No permanent replacement was ever found for Horace, but Cornelia did manage to find a new church, one that was progressive in ways that would have astounded its Presbyterian founders. In the early seventies when Cornelia joined, her new congregation was like a flock of enraged geese—aggressive not only in chasing away sin but in the pursuit of new converts, especially in the fertile battleground of the Third World, where charismatic evangelicals were stealing a march to the Lord's thunder. Cornelia's Presbyterians responded with full-scale recruitment drives. She was among the ready volunteers willing to seek front-line action, but her still-recent conversion made her suspect, and she was assigned instead to Kitchen Patrol.

Cornelia filled in the trough left by Horace with involvement; does it matter if her altruism was tinted with grief when she undertook to foster a motherless child in faraway Guyana? She was one of the few willing to back her financial contribution with an investment of time and emotion in the programs of her church.

Each One Teach One was one of the most successful Outreach Programs that the Presbyterian Church ever undertook. Canadian congregations were twinned with missions in the Third World; members were given every opportunity to become directly involved in the activities of their missions. In general, participation was limited to donations in return for photographic evidence of progress: children screaming after life-saving injections, or smiling delight for the camera in hand-me-down clothes, exporting earnestness from crowded classrooms, holding up books—education, like a talisman to invoke promise and exorcise guilt. But Each One Teach One also opened up opportunities on both sides, for empty vessels longing to be filled by those touched with the eager fever of impossible dreams.

Cornelia's interest in her foster child, Buphendra, sustained. She shared her lifelong passion for reading with him: books were a bridge—a common denominator that reduced the years between them and the miles apart. She delighted in his discoveries and keenly felt his disappointments as he grew in her heart from foster child to friend, from child to man.

And Cornelia worked her way out of the church kitchen up to the phone-lines, from volunteer secretary to paid Administrative Assistant, from Coordinator of Special Events to Regional Director of Outreach Programs. No one will openly accuse her, and even those who whisper forgive her for using her influence to help her one time foster child land a scholarship. Eyebrows were raised but no objections voiced when she rearranged her tour of the Missions to coincide with his departure from Guyana. After all those crusading years in the trenches, Cornelia is at last airborne and on her way to the front—her sense of mission intact, taking with her from among all the good advice only a few books to read and a little ray of hope.

～

"BP? Wake up. Wake up, BP! Today is the day when your Great White Mother comes to take you away from me. I know how you will soon forget me, once you make your way across water. I know that in my heart. When you gone you gone. But BP, wake up. Wake up, BP, and give me one more loveup."

"Shush, Minoo, don't talk like that," BP blots away her tears with his kisses. "You know I will send for you. As soon as everything fixup, I will send for you, Minoo."

"BP, don't play the poor fool damn fool with me and my heart." Minoo will take only one kind of consoling, "Come and give me one more loveup. Then is gone you gone."

BP lives underneath the cube on stilts that is his uncle's house. He has built a room of his own; from three pillars, with bricks and a little mortar, he has cornered a space for his bed and his precious books—privacy.

Minoo has her ear to his heart. BP inhales the fragrance of her hair. Minoo memorizes his every touch. A little bit of moon becomes bold like the sun for an instant ... then clouds over, and from those clouds—teardrops.

"What sort of thing is this love?" Minoo wants to know, "How it can wet you down but parch me up so?"

BP has no answer to this riddle. Today is the day that he has waited on for most of the twenty-one years of his life; who can blame him if he is more eager to say hello to the future than goodbye to the past?

"Minoo girl, is best you hurry and go back home now, before daybreak. Before your mammy miss you out." BP fishes around for his Jockey shorts; with a scrap of soap and little else, he makes a dash for the rain barrel.

Minoo is seventeen, and heavy with the for-certain knowledge that a life without love is not worth living, but not even that can slow her down as she moves with the quick steps of someone who is sure of the way, overtaking sure-footed goats that stray down the slope of the hill to the unfenced boundary of the main road, past a coop of hens that cluck at her, not with sympathy but with the sideways gossiping looks that she sees every day too often. Who is this poor fool damn fool Minoo? Why is she throwing herself away on that boy who long time all the time studying and making big man plans? Quite a few of those chickens will have their necks wrung this morning, and one of those goats will lose its head from a sharp stroke with a cutlass and end up in a curry, on a bed of the best basmati rice, in front of the Great White Mother.

This far upcountry, the main road is little more than two lanes of loose gravel with the tell-tale swatches of asphalt that always appear just before an election. (You can tell who is voting for whom by whose driveway gets slicked.) Minoo crosses the road, down into the gully where her father has chosen to perch his box of a house, up on stilts, like some sort of clumsy wading bird. A kerosene lamp is on in the kitchen, like an eye, watching and waiting, for who? Poor fool damn fool is who.

Every year, some up-country girl does drink insecticide and make the newspapers, for the sake of love. A love that tears her up inside. It have girls who does pray for love to at least leave a baby behind for them to mind, but all love does leave those poor fools with is a broken heart. Minoo makes a determined vow: that is not going to happen to her; love has played the damn fool for the first and the last time with her heart.

Minoo wipes but her tears won't stop. She sets her face and her mind to the argument ahead. She will pretend, but convince no one, that her tears are nothing more than a little morning dew. Then she will recall a little bit of comfort gleaned from her most favourite of movie stars, Ranjit Ragoonanan: "A broken heart will mend. It is better to suffer from a broken heart … than to lose your whole head."

~

"Minoo! Minoo! Come quick Minoo!"

BP has raced all the way down the hill from his room to hers; in the evening dark and in his haste, he has stepped in some fresh asphalt and ruined his new shoes. These are his going-away shoes, after years of false starts and dashed expectations, he is a trip to the airport away from leaving Guyana at last.

Now is not the time to be stuck like a tar baby; now is his time to reap. He has sowed so many careful seeds; he has nurtured his hopes in this white woman for years. But why she must come all the way from Canada to fall down sick? What else could go wrong?

BP frantically wipes his new shoes.

"BP? What you come and call me for?" Minoo yells back, out her window.

"Come and help me out. Minoo, please." BP begs. "The white lady sick—"

"—BP? What you think I is? Your servant girl? You think I must come and clean up after your white lady? Do you know what they're saying about you man?" Minoo comes outside and catches up to a worried BP.

"They're saying that you are a fast worker. 'Look how that white lady only reach Uplands a few hours ago and already she in BP's bed!'"

"Shush! Don't talk like that, Minoo," BP scolds her. "You yourself see how poorly she was feeling. She went for a little lie-down and now she gone and vomit up the place. She not used to this kind of climate."

"I think is more the dark rum and the curry goat what knock she down," Minoo's laugh is full of spite.

BP is too worried to fight spite with scorn. "Minoo, if you not willing to help, tell me now—"

"No—BP." Minoo overtakes him. "People done breezing they mouth plenty enough on you and she already. I will come."

"You think I have those damn fools to study?" BP finds his scorn. "Soon I will be gone, and I will never have to hear that pack of jackasses bray again."

"When you gone you gone. Yes, that is true." Minoo's sorrow overtakes her scorn. "You have plenty book sense, BP, but for a big man it have plenty you still don't know. You was right to call me. I must be the one to go and look after your white lady."

A relieved BP agrees, "Come come, Minoo. Come let we go—"

"—No." Minoo turns a window into a door. "You go and fetch a basin of clean water, bring some Limacol, and see if your uncle have any cloves in the house."

~

Limes. Cloves. Coconut oil. Asphalt of course. And ... sex.

Cornelia takes inventory with her nose. She can remember innumerable warnings to keep her eyes open and her wits about her at all times, but she cannot recall being given a single piece of advice or one word of warning about her nose. Yet from the minute she stepped off the airplane in Guyana, on the last leg of her trip, the first strike against her sensory system was launched not by the explosion of noise or the scorching heat, but by the rioting smells from warring food vendors.

The long drive up-country to the Mission, in the equatorial heat, on a scratch of a road that winced like a fresh scar through the jungle, escalated the assault on Cornelia's senses. The feast held in her honour by Buphendra's family completed the rout.

Cornelia threw up and fainted. But now that her nausea and the accompanying giddiness has stopped, her nose is working overtime to restore some sense of order to her surroundings.

Asphalt is easy. The smell of it is everywhere. It seems to get right into the lungs. Initially it seems harsh and abrasive, but Cornelia has decided that it is an optimistic smell, bracing.

Cloves is more of a taste than a smell. A numbness around her mouth. No, in the sour taste of her mouth, Cornelia locates a small stick of clove up under her lip, pressed up against her gums.

Limes. The scent of limes, mixed with what? Alcohol? In perfume? On her skin, someone has applied a splash of coolness against her temples and on her wrists.

Coconut oil is a new scent for her. She first noticed it emanating from the hair and skin of women, young and old, at the meal, at the enormous feast, held in her honour by Buphendra's family. It is a broad scent, more persistent than insistent, and yet subtle in that it takes on the aspect of each wearer. In this room, it is on the pillow, in the sheets, and it is mingled, conjoined with, male and female, dark and warm, now pungent and unmistakable, the odours of sexual congress.

The rebellion of her senses launches another sharp regional attack, from her upset stomach down to her groin. Cornelia recalls an observation first noted after Horace died: It is possible to have desire without an object, but it is a bland fruit—all water, no sugar.

Her sexual arousal is unwanted, unwilled, and like everything about this place, unexpected. There is barely time to get used to one wild juxtaposition before another superimposes itself: plants that are impossibly delicate with flowers that are positively carnal ... men in T-shirts, jiggling advertisements on bellies, next to artfully costumed women in saris handmade from exquisite silk ... the subtle flavours of cardamom and coriander set on fire with lethal chilies and washed down with the most potent rum ... sitting down to a marvelous meal in open eyesight of goats fornicating, fornicating with abandon.

The scent of abandon...

~

"I don't like how she looking. And look how she breathing, shallow shallow. You think I should wake she up?" BP is relieved to have Minoo take charge, but he doesn't like it. "I think I'll send for the doctor, yes."

"No," Minoo has taken complete charge. "Leave her be. Your white lady is young for a Great White Mother, but she still have some age on her, you know. She look as if she could use a little rest. That is all. If you want to make yourself useful, go over to the Mission House. Tell them how she feeling poorly. Let the white people come and look after their own. Tell them to send the Land Rover for she.

"What you waiting for?" Minoo can't resist a swipe at BP. "I know how is ready you done ready to go. Go and see if they want to move up the arrangements for the drive to the airport."

"Shush, Minoo. You don't have to be like that." Buphendra continues to hover over Cornelia. He is reluctant to leave and let her out of his sight: he is afraid that the thin thread on which his entire future hangs will unravel.

Cornelia separates the whispers; she attaches the coconut oil and the scent of sex that envelops her to the girl—Minoo. Buphendra never mentioned her in his letters. This should not be so surprising, but it is. So much about Buphendra, starting with his nick-name, Bee Pee, is a surprise. It is the only informal thing about him.

Buphendra she knows something about, but this BP—he is a stranger. When the scholarship came through, but with reduced funding, Cornelia felt that she knew Buphendra well enough to offer him, without any reservations, a place in her home. But now she wonders, what can you really know about someone from years of letter writing, augmented with the occasional poorly taken photograph?

Buphendra is so stiff, and he is so guarded, like someone with a secret to betray. His reticence stands out all the more because everyone else has been so brazen: a curious mixture of the blatant and the sly that would be alarming, if they weren't all so disarmingly obvious.

The whispering drifts away. Buphendra is in profile, in the

doorway. He is a handsome man, slight but not small, with even features, except for a generous nose which is kept in perspective by a square broom of a mustache. He does not stand out but apart, in his immaculate white shirt and khaki pants as opposed to everyone else's T-shirts and blue denim. And there is something military in his posture—every hair in his mustache is so precisely clipped. Obviously intelligent, and the inquisitiveness is still there … but nothing else is left of the boy whose innocence and exuberance at every discovery so captivated and delighted Cornelia.

How much of his strangeness should she discount to her growing sense of displacement? Cornelia's tour of the Missions was supposed to make her, the new never-travelled Regional Director of Outreach Programs, cognizant of all the 'real work' being done in the field. The pervasive philosophy behind the Missions is that we are all God's children; work in the Missions is not only God's business … it is high up on His agenda, but every stop along her route has undermined assumptions and convictions deeply held.

Cornelia has seen how the idea of the 'global village' is now taken for fact: it informs all of the programs directed at the Missions. But all the evidence of her trip says that it does not exist. Fads and fashions, the icons of commerce, have created a superficial verisimilitude—but as soon as you exit the cities, leave the portals of trade and it is both immediate and apparent that there is a great divide. On the narrow road out to the Mission, the impatient way of the Land Rover sent to transport her was blocked for nearly an hour by a cart drawn by a plodding ox. Her driver shook his head in resigned frustration and pointed to a new tractor rusting idle in a nearby field. Everywhere Cornelia looked, there were signs that it is just as easy to abandon as it is to believe.

Is Buphendra a believer? Or is he among those who so easily abandon? His room offers Cornelia no clues of BP the man. His books are all in boxes, all evidence of Buphendra the boy and their shared discoveries packed for donation to the Mission. Cornelia twists and turns in the bed sheets, to the source of the coconut oil scent.

"How you feeling? Madam? How you feeling?"

Cornelia sorts for an appropriate response, and she discovers with some surprise that she is tongue-tied.

Minoo ventures closer and asks again, "Madam?"

"…Cloves?" Cornelia manages a question.

"Cloves does tie up the tongue, madam." Minoo supplies.

"In case it was a stroke you was having. A tie up tongue," Minoo explains further, "is hard to swallow."

Cornelia sits up in BP's bed. "The limes?"

"Limacol," Minoo passes the bottle. "You don't have this up in Canada? BP should make sure and take some with him."

Cornelia takes a whiff of the Limacol. "No, I'm sure I would have remembered this scent."

"Limacol good for fever, madam." Minoo offer her opinion on Cornelia's condition: "I believe that what you have is an ague. The best thing for ague is herbs in a hot-water bath."

"I could use a good soak." Cornelia's attempt at a smile is more weak than brave, as she tries to get up.

"No no, no madam, you take it easy," Minoo insists. "Let me give you a cowboy. And you will feel better."

"A what?" Cornelia asks.

Minoo giggles, "You ever see how those cowboys does take a bath in the movies? Whoosh! Whoosh! They done and they gone."

"I see," Cornelia says. She feels exposed, as if her desire is a spilled secret, out in the open, like the other scents that fill the room.

"Where's Buphendra?" Cornelia gathers the bedsheets about herself.

"BP gone to the Mission House to organize a drop." Minoo fetches the basin, wets a cloth, and begins to wipe Cornelia's face. "He soon come back."

Cornelia is a woman who long ago, by the dint of insistence, stamped out any attempts to call her Nell, Nelly, or any other much-detested abbreviation. She has been called aloof and prudish; she readily admits to being reserved and proper; being attended to, especially in this aroused state of unfocused desire, embarrasses her. Menopause comes early to the women in her family; perhaps that is all it is—a flare—a first signal. She is able to will her arousal away, and attribute its tingling residue to the earlier warmth, to the path of the chilies.

Minoo swabs the washcloth down Cornelia's neck and under her blouse, to do her armpits and the hollow between her breasts. Cornelia is startled but makes no protest or attempt to stop her. After the cowboy, Minoo produces a vial of her coconut oil. She tilts Cornelia's head back and begins to apply the scented oil in small overlapping circles to Cornelia's neck and face.

When? Has she ever been catered to like this? Cornelia feels something between complicity and compliance, as she makes the small adjustments of her body that allow Minoo to continue her ministrations. She has the distinct impression that she is being massaged into position by Minoo.

Minoo has satisfied some of her curiosity: the white lady is flesh and bones just like anybody. It have one or two widows in Uplands with insurance money, but they owe their status to someone else, much like the wives of the teachers at the Mission. BP is not the only one up on his toes around the white lady; everybody at the Mission has tried their best to curry the Great White Mother's favor. There is no question about Cornelia's importance, but Minoo is a little disappointed with her up close inspection. The movies are her chief source of information and inspiration: she half expected half hoped that Cornelia would have some sort of 'star quality.'

"Madam, you would not believe how BP used to look forward to those books you used to send for him. BP's nose was always in a book. People say how BP is a damn fool dreamer. BP have brains for so, but when it comes to ordinary common-sense, BP never got his share."

"Many men seem to have that problem," Cornelia says dryly.

"Madam, that is the truth for true," Minoo giggles, and then she adds in the ingratiatingly sly tone that Cornelia has come to recognize, "It have people who say how BP have a big head. How he have big ambition. But, I think, for a man, that is not such a bad thing to have."

Ambition? Is that all it is? Cornelia considers a dozen ways to put her reservations about Buphendra into a question and rejects them all. She has invited a friend into her house but a stranger is coming instead. If a way across the divide, a way out of Guyana, was all that Buphendra wanted from her friendship, the pragmatist in Cornelia says that he has earned it, but the foster parent who invested so much long distance hope in him is palpably disappointed.

"Madam? How you feeling now?" Minoo continues to massage Cornelia's neck and shoulders. "You feel any better, madam?"

What are you looking for? Cornelia turns her attention to Minoo. What sly plan have you hatched? What are you seeking to abandon? But instead of questions, Cornelia stiffens, "Much better, thank you."

Skepticism is the learned lesson of Cornelia's trip, it has been reinforced by example into cynicism, by Buphendra, and by all who are so piously certain as they go busily about God's business, secure in the belief that they are 'better people for it,' and the knowledge that theirs is 'a tour of duty' and it will end.

Cornelia, who is both eager and anxious to return home to the security of Canada, indulges in some soul searching. Is she to be numbered among those who abandon now?

Minoo's fingers detect the change in Cornelia. White people too damn funny, yes. Why they does always have to talk from the side of their mouth? Minoo pours more coconut oil, and she does her fatalistic best to keep her heart from breaking by keeping her fingers busy.

Cornelia is not attuned to it, but Minoo has been listening for it, and she is acutely aware of a new note, added to the insect noises of the night: the Land Rover will be here in a very few minutes.

"Madam, I is the only woman that BP ever know." Minoo

shares her only secret, "I even try and make baby with him. But I see now that not even that could keep him from you."

And now you are pregnant? Is that it? Cornelia keeps her eyes tightly closed. She refuses to be drawn in, to even look at Minoo.

"My BP is a damn fool, you know," Minoo starts to cry, "but he is a sweet sweet fool."

"Madam…" Minoo's voice falters. "I is glad for BP. But I is afraid for BP, in a big place like Canada."

"Madam please… you will look out for him, for me?"

"I'm sure Buphendra will write you," Cornelia offers. But she is already sure that once he reaches Canada, Buphendra will skip, once—twice, and then he will vanish, he will sink like a stone without a trace.

Minoo tries her best but she can't stop; she turns away from Cornelia to do her crying over by the door.

"When he gone he gone. I knows that in my heart."

There is finality in Minoo's voice that touches a hollow place inside Cornelia; it forces her to look. How could she not notice that this girl Minoo is little more than a child? If she is more transparent than sly, is it because she is so young? Or is it because … Cornelia remembers well this sound of loss, of first love lost. If we are not all God's children under the skin, Cornelia sighs, then at least we are in the flesh.

Cornelia would like to reach for Minoo and steer her gently around, to sit her down on BP's bed, next to her, and offer her some comfort. But what comfort will it be to know that a hurt like this does not stop? Time will blunt it, but it never goes entirely away. And if she is indeed pregnant, what will she have?

The fruit? Or a thorn of love? What can she console Minoo with? The future? What hope does the future hold for a Minoo? And what hope is there for her child? A new Buphendra who will have the slender thread of an absent father to spin dreams around.

Cornelia wobbles out of Buphendra's bed to join Minoo at the door. It has been explained to her, the curve of the earth, the nearness to the equator, but Cornelia is always surprised at the way night falls in the tropics, so sudden and so final. Together, they listen to the approach, for the high-metal note of a Land Rover.

BIENVENUE AU CANADA

*A*RRET.

I am at the airport.

Access interdict. Arrivees.

The International Airport.

I park my car somewhere deep in the colon of the Parkade, under a sign that says: REMEMBER YOUR LEVEL. (Good advice is everywhere.)

This is what I like and hate about airports: The magic way doors open and close without you touching them and, once inside, the instant-coffee dissolve to nervous and expectant. Why do they call these places terminals when they are a communist swirl of anonymity, modular plastic, and rootless plants growing in sunless confusion?

The locus of my nervousness is in my jacket pocket; over my heart, in my wallet, is a letter from Lily. Flight Number, Date and Time of Arrival, in her neat handwriting. I've pored over this cryptogram for two weeks and I have decoded nothing. Credits scroll by on the overhead monitors. I am on the set of a thousand reunions. I rehearse my opening lines. But I have no idea what script we will follow.

~

Please fasten your seatbelts.

Obey the No Smoking signs.
We're about to begin our final descent.

I never liked this flight, this connection, Georgetown to Port of Spain to Toronto. I hate the stopover; those Trinidadians know how to make you suffer. If you're flying in from Guyana they treat you like a cockroach; they want to mash you to the ground and then twist their foot on your back.

And God help you if you are a woman travelling alone, and you end up seated next to a Trini man. His wife could be in the very next seat and still he will feel obligated to offer you his sexual services. Only one thing is worse … the Trini woman. They all act as if they have a license to probe and inspect the intimate apparel of your life.

It is my misfortune to be seated next to not one, but two: a mother and her daughter. The flight is nearly over and this is the first bit of peace and quiet for me. Mother, with daughter in tow, went off to the washroom. Daughter is going up to Toronto to start university. Mother is along to see her 'business fixup good good,' to make sure that 'my girlchild don't end up living in no nastiness.'

My God, the scared, eager look on that girl's face brought back so many memories. I started to tell Daughter what it was like for me when I first went up to university in Canada. Mother gave me one cut-eye, a sharp, skeptical look, as if to say: Who is you?

A very good question.

I am Lily Seecharan-Carew, the first married woman in Georgetown to almost keep her maiden name. Even for this hyphenated compromise I had to fight Johnny. He couldn't stand for his wife, couldn't stand for the public to see that he had a wife with a mind of her own. Johnny preached liberation when we were at York. "Up country people won't—can't understand." He quickly reconverted once we got back home.

~

A huge crowd is waiting for Lily's flight. Greeks, Italians, and the Portuguese have this in common with West Indians: they all have a thing for airport reunions. Everybody shows up: babies barely outside the womb, old people with one foot in the grave, friends and neighbours who migrated years ago and only vaguely remember the new arrival still come to bear witness.

I have not seen Lily in almost six years. Not since she finished her practicum. She went straight back to Guyana. And got married.

Lily is a widow now.

Aldwin Poon, one of the few people I keep up with from university days, was the one who called and told me about Johnny See. "Andrew? You hear boy? You hear about Johnny See? Johnny See get mashup."

He had read about it in the alumni magazine. Johnny See got a feature obit. That is how I heard about Johnny Seecharan's death. That is how I always and ever heard about Johnny See, after the fact. He was always a rogue planet (revise that to meteorite) pulling things out of orbit.

~

We came straight from school in Canada, got married right away, and went upcountry. Johnny had to work off his scholarship. Two years. Johnny had me sold on his idyllic vision of the schoolteacher and the doctor: it soon clashed with the dried and whitened cow dung on the *ajoupa* floor.

When I told him how uncomfortable living upcountry made me feel, Johnny laughed. He said I had spent too much of my time at York, 'reading Romantic poets, too much Plato and not enough Hobbes.'

After the first two years, Johnny extended his contract for one more year. I begged, he promised, and we compromised: we would stay but only until the rains came. When the next dry season came and met us still upcountry, I refused. No more for me. I went back to Georgetown.

Georgetown was even worse than upcountry; it betrays so many promises. 'Outages', 'interruptions', and 'shortages' made the brief patches when things worked the way they should seem miraculous. Our marriage followed a similar pattern. I complained bitterly and always compared how we were living with how we could be living up in Canada.

Johnny said he was building a base upcountry; he said he had political ambitions, but most of that was rumshop talk. We bought a big house in a good area just outside Georgetown. And I became The Doctor's Wife.

I got a teaching position at the same Girls' Catholic School that I had attended. My other job was to keep the big house running smoothly. And to entertain important and rising political stars lavishly, on my teacher's salary, on the weekends when Johnny came to town.

Johnny Seecharan thrived up country, where incidents and accidents are quickly converted into legends and myths. Go to Georgetown today and go anywhere up country from there—people are still talking about the night Johnny See crashed.

He foretold his own death of course, in joking conversations eerily recalled. In a string of rumshops men who drank only scotch mourned the loss of one of their own. His wake lasted for three days. No glass was ever empty. Fire one. Fire one more. Fire one for Johnny See. Fire down at thiry-one in a car crash.

The rainy season turns everything to muck so quickly, upcountry.

~

I first heard about Johnny See from my parents, long before I ever met him. My parents were both Presbyterian Ministers; they made a career of carrying a little learning and the Good Word into remote places.

We lived in Guyana the longest. The first time for five years. Then my parents were recalled to Canada; the political climate in Guyana was unsettled. And there was also some political infighting going on in the Presbyterian Overseas Outreach Program.

The wife of the couple sent to replace my parents couldn't cope. She contracted what my parents called a "topical disease". My parents were sent back to Guyana to finish up the contract. I stayed behind in Canada to finish up my school year.

When I got back to Guyana, Johnny See had been and gone. He came from upcountry to Georgetown to take his A-Levels; he went up to Canada on a full scholarship, to study medicine.

My parents said he was the best and brightest student they had ever taught.

That second stint in Guyana was when I first met Lily. She was Lily Carew then. We were both getting ready to go to university in Canada. We did a lot of talking and handholding. We taught each other how to kiss. Whenever the conversation slowed, we would work on our kissing.

My parents had me put my name in for a bursary through our church; I got it under the condition that I attend Laurentian, in Sudbury. Lily went to York.

We wrote. We both skipped lunches to pay for long-distance calls. I took the bus down to Toronto to see her three times. Lily came up to Sudbury once.

It was during the week after Christmas, from Boxing Day to New Year's Eve. It was freezing cold in Sudbury. It was her first Christmas away. And we had the handy privacy of my room. We did much more than kiss. But it's not just that we made love. I know that for at least that one week, Lily loved me.

The next time I came down from Sudbury to York, there was a Caribbean Students' Association dance. Lily had the flu but insisted on going. I was ready to leave at any time, but Lily wanted to stay just a little bit longer.

It was well past midnight when Johnny See showed up, high as a kite, with an entourage of loud and proud drinkers.

We were introduced: "Hey Johnny See, you long streak of misery, come and meet a fellow Guyanese; meet a man who is a Guyanese by proxy."

Johnny See had the talent, the ability to remain lucid while drunk. He said he knew my parents well; he even called them by their first names. No one under fifty ever dared to call my parents by their first names.

Johnny asked, then he whisked a suddenly eager Lily off to dance. When she finally returned, her face was flushed and her eyes were bright and shining.

I continued to write and phone. As soon as school finished, Lily went home to Guyana for the summer. I stayed in Sudbury to work for my tuition and a transfer to York.

I got to York in September. Way too late.

Lily and I spent a year avoiding each other. Things changed when she started living with Johnny See, and I stopped hanging out exclusively with West Indians and made some Canadian friends. I realized that I had no 'back home' to return to, Canada was it. By third year, it was okay for us to have coffee together again. When I began to have doubts about becoming a teacher, it was Lily who talked me through.

I never learned to like Johnny See. I admired his intelligence and I envied his verve. I think he liked me; he accepted me as Lily's friend. I don't think he ever saw me as a threat, and I never fooled myself into thinking that I was or could be.

About one Sunday a month Lily would invite me over. After supper, Lily would pick a topic to initiate our 'discussions'. Johnny See looked forward to these discussions that nearly always dissolved into heated arguments. We all did. Women's Lib and Guyanese politics were big favourites, but we ranged far and everything was fair game. Johnny had absolutely no qualms about employing any and all rhetorical weapons. He would make personal attacks on your character if he felt that would give him an edge. When he wanted to be dismissive, he would call me a "neo-colonial hybrid." He could reduce Lily to tears with the same skill he possessed as a surgeon. Sometimes he would cut too deep and bring out a side of her that was always a shock to me. Lily could curse and swear with the best.

One of those Sundays, we got on to the topic of love. Johnny See said, "Love alone is not enough." It was the first and only time we all three agreed, but I don't think any of us were talking about the same thing.

~

It never stopped raining once. Until five minutes before Johnny's funeral.

They came from far off: upcountry girls, young and thin like cane in arrow, cotton dresses damp with handprints; red eyes in not-so-innocent faces showed where Johnny See passed. The bent and the mended, all those who "got a patchup from the Doc," talked of the deep scar of his passing. The Boys' Presbyterian School let out early for Johnny See; nurses from the hospital, still in uniform, scattered kerchiefs in the crowd. Johnny's friends from high-school days, from university, some in Government, and those out of favour with whom he hatched plot and counterplot—a wide circle of young immortals suddenly old—gathered close in black shirt-jacks and shades, under a weak-tea sky, sharing the same mirrored look.

And, Johnny's family.

The men I never saw, a wolf pack, scattered to lick their collective wound and choose a new leader. The women filled my house with strange smells from my kitchen, packed up his clothes and his books, took down photographs … wrapped me in a sari, took a hold of my elbow, steered me to the edge, and handed me a clump of earth to cast and deflect off the polished mahogany casket with the window, for Johnny See…

∾

I started missing Lily months before they left to go back to Guyana.

One day we went for coffee. After the coffee, we went walking in what felt like the worst winter weather in the history of the world. I had to tell her how I felt.

"Lily, I'm sorry," I said, "but I can't stop myself. Everywhere I look, I see you pass. Mornings, I'm sure it's you in the pack on the bus. In the grocery, I know it's you down at the end of the aisle. I'm going to give myself whiplash. I can't stand the thought of never seeing you again. But in a way, I wish you were gone already."

Lily took my hand and we walked some more. I thought Lily started to laugh; then I felt her starting to cry. We stopped. I didn't know what more to say, so I kissed her. She hesitated, but then she kissed me back.

And we kissed. Clouds of kisses … until the winter air was blue about our faces.

∾

I continued to live in the big house with the sweet scent of roses, but with a new role: The Doctor's Widow. Johnny See would have laughed at the irony. During the week when Johnny was away, I had to fend off the most brazen advances from his friends. On his death, they abandoned all of their lechery and innuendo, and they elected me keeper of his shrine. I felt buried alive with a pharaoh. Covered in guilt. (If only… if I had only stayed with him upcountry, Johnny wouldn't have been rushing back and forth from work to rumshop to Georgetown on weekends.)

The cards and letters kept coming. Long after the fact, the news would boomerang back to the mailbox in envelopes of disbelief from far places in the hearts that Johnny touched: staff in the hospital where he did his residency, the landlord of the basement suite where we lived in Toronto, classmates and professors—all wrote of their sadness at the loss of so much potential.

Andrew wrote.

A short, sweet, tentative note. He told me to have courage, in that halting, awkward way of his. His letter made me think of winter, of Canada—the bracing cold, the anonymous order. I put off writing him back. He wrote again. He gave me his telephone number and said if I ever felt like it to call, collect. I sent him a card at Christmas. He managed to get fresh flowers delivered to me on my birthday.

Johnny's family sent a delegation to insist I come and go upcountry for a visit. I went for a weekend to star in a comedy of errors. They made a match for me with one of Johnny's cousins, a young lawyer. They made it very clear that he was quite a catch for an aging widow like me.

Johnny, you always said, "We only make the choices that we can live with." Why couldn't I settle back into the lurching insolvency of Guyana like you? With you. Canada was a red flag that

I waved between us, at our marriage. For that I feel guilt; for that, Johnny See, I am sorry. But of all the things that I have felt in my life, regret is the worst.

That Sunday night, as soon as I got back to Georgetown I sat down and wrote Andrew a letter. I told him I was coming up to Toronto for a visit. And I asked if he could meet me at the airport.

~

A flashing relay on the overhead monitor says that Lily's flight has just landed. The crowd of greeters surges towards the glass sliding doors. There is movement behind, of officials, and a false start of expectancy as a maintenance crew emerges.

It's so irrational, how I still feel. It's been six years. Will she even recognize me? Now I can't remember even one of my carefully rehearsed lines. I'm with my back secure against a pillar and eyes front. All of my expectations are trained on those doors that open by magic.

~

I like Andrew. I like his decency.

I think he still loves me.

I care, but can I ever love him? With all of my heart?

Mesdames et Messieurs.
We have just landed.
Bienvenue au Canada.

JES GREW

*"It belonged to nobody, its words were unprintable
but its tune irresistible."*
   —From *Mumbo Jumbo* by Ishamael Reed

"SAD EYES GONE Ras! I'm telling you!" Verna shouts as soon as the elevator door opens. This scoop was just too hot for Verna; it couldn't keep in her apartment. Verna couldn't wait, she had to go and greet Denise with it down by the elevator.

"Child," Denise steps out from inside a Rubik's cube full of people, "What Sad Eyes know 'bout Rasta?" The elevator door closes, leaving those inside to go on up with this puzzling snippet unsolved.

Denise can feel the boom-a-doom boom-a-doom pulse of reggae playing the way it should, bass cranked up high and hard, threatening, dishes shivering from percussion in the kitchen cupboards.

"Girl, your mother landlord must be praying for the lease to finish."

"She don't higgle him on the rent. That's all he cares 'bout."

Verna lives so high up, Denise can't stand it. But she likes the view.

"Those white people must be mad, playing tennis down there in this hot sun." Denise shakes her head.

"Come and give me the rake," Denise laughs. "Sad Eyes playing in his tail. What Sad Eyes know 'bout Rasta?"

"Girl, he coming over this evening. For dreadlocks."

"Child," Denise cackles, "Sad Eyes playing man. His mother go roast his tail. You locks-up she son head and is You and She.

She and You. She go come for—You!"

Verna studies her own hair in the bathroom mirror before brandishing a curling iron; each wave of her wand gives off an electric sizzle on contact with the globs of gel damping down her hair. It's a lot of work to get the *look* right.

"I'm putting something else on," Denise yells from the living room.

"Let my reggae finish!" Verna screams as she miscues with the curling iron.

"Reggae Rhythm is out," Denise states, "O-U-T."

"Ohnoohno," Verna refutes in a chorus from the bathroom. "Roots reggae still going strong," but her feet and hips reset and engage automatically in synch to the new music that Denise selects.

~

Check him out. Check him out.

Sad Eyes is contorted into a position attainable only by teen-agers: parts of one leg and an elbow must be somehow suc-tioned to the bed, his other elbow rests on the floor, the hand attached to it props open a large book, the top of his head swivels along as he turns the pages.

Sad Eyes is focused on the Emperor of Ethiopia. He admires the WWII vintage picture of his Royal Highness, the King of Kings, Conquering Lion of the tribe of Judah, Ras Haile Selassie I, in full dress uniform, in exile.

Check him out! Check him out!

He scans the column of words offsetting the Emperor's

picture, but it's all a dim blur to Sad Eyes; Churchill-Mussolini rings as one faint grade nine World Affairs bell. He sets aside the big library book on Africa that's his source and fires up a cigarette, pretending it's a joint; drawing fresh inspiration in through his mouth, he practices holding it in … in case, then spluttering out his nostrils.

He is a man-lion in an Africa glimpsed from grainy movies and picture books, a rehash that would make Tarzan blanch and slink away. Two anatomically correct, actual-size, naked pygmy females are stalking him with long spears. They stop about six feet in front of him and cross their spears to form an X entrance, waving him through. On a long march, the tall grasslands grow dense with trees and twining vines that hang down curl up into upside-down question marks. Snakes alive! His escorts vanish without a trace. The jungle swallows him whole. He blinks away beads of sweat and looks wide-eyed around now, for any clue, any sign.

The tree cover is so thick and matted overhead that the sky's blue is completely lost and there's a green underwater feel to the air. He's having trouble breathing. Each and every sound is amplified, tuned to his racing heartbeat and an incessant background drumming, until one metallic groan jars him—a long fingernail scratch against a blackboard, followed by a machine growl. He recognizes the engine of his mom's car, coming home from work, then another scratch as the automatic garage door closes.

Goodbye Africa. He flaps his arms frantically, waving the cigarette smell away, opens a window, stuffs his books on Africa under his socks, makes a few more furtive teenage stabs at tidying up his room, dashes to the washroom for a Listerine rinse, and answers his mom's—"Hello? Are you there?"— between gargles.

~

"Talk to him. George, I want you to talk to him."

George replies with a ring of resignation and an echo of old arguments, "It's just growing pains the boy having."

"You hear me?" Shirley continues, "I want you to talk to him man to man. I eh able nah. He don't listen to me. It don't do no good. This afternoon, before I could catch myself, I give him one lash. Hard upside him head, but all he do is laugh at me. Him head hard. You must talk to him, man to man."

"All right Shirley, all right."

"I don't like him smoking. I don't want him smoking. But if him must smoke, I don't want him doing it in my house. Tell him that. For me."

"Let me finish eat nuh," George concentrates on his black-eyed peas, picking and probing them out from his rice, shepherding them off to the side of his plate, one by one, herding them behind a stringy semicolon of salt pork.

See how life funny, George reads from his arrangement of peas, see how things does take a turn. When they first got married, he was well comfortable in Oakville; it was Shirley who beg, come go, come go out west, to Calgary. And she had to beg hard again, before they move to Red Deer. Now, is he who have the hotfoot to move but no matter how hard he beg, Shirley chants at him as if she praying from a rosary—how she eh moving from this house, how the boy need to settle once and for all in school, how she like the church here although they can't sing worth a fart, and how is high time they settle down and plant some roots in Canada, once and for all.

George can feel something riding up and down his stomach; he accuses and convicts the black-eyed peas. The boy is fifteen, he playing man already, he even have woman, he can handle himself, what it have left to tell him? Six years ago, when George married Shirley, he never had expectations to be a father to the boy, never. But he had hopes.

"I can't finish this nuh," George clatters into the kitchen with his plate.

Shirley stops loading the dishwasher and straightens her back, one hand on her kidneys the other cocked; she sports the same look that Marvin Hagler used to get, a look that says, come, I am ready for you.

George scrapes his plate and escapes with a beer to his sanctuary in the garage. He unfolds a week's worth of Trinidad Sunday papers sent religiously from back home by his sister. George likes his cricket, and it's hard to get any cricketing news in Canada. When the newspapers arrived, he used to head straight for the Sports section. Now he makes a beeline to and lingers over the classifieds, comparing house prices, converting dollars in job advertisements, minus inflation, plus cost of living—he fine-tunes his figures with each shipment of papers. In another column of his mind, he keeps a running inventory of what Shirley points to whenever he tries to broach the subject of going back.

"Man, you must be mad," is her standard reply. "Why you

think we come up to Canada in the first damn place? We could never in a million years live like this back there. Look man, you in charge of white people where you working. And look how we have two cars done paid for, another few years please God, we go own this house, dishwasher, microwave oven and all."

George works in the oil patch. His job is to drill for and map sour gas reservoirs. Sometimes when you drill and hit a pocket of gas, you can't cap the damn thing and it comes bubbling up everywhere: a job ad cut out from the newspapers his sister sends, for Drillers, is yellowing around in his wallet; tucked away in a garage drawer is a business card from an overseas mover. Everything has a sour gas taste now, even Shirley's cooking; those black-eyed peas looked as if they were looking to burst out of their jackets.

～

"Where you going, Mister man?"

"By Verna."

"What you doing going by Verna? That girl too old for you."

"Mom, she' s only eighteen."

"Three years is plenty when you only have fifteen."

"Yeah, right."

"Don't smart-mouth with me, Jeffery. And what you screw-ing up your face for? What?"

"I hate that name."

"Jefferson is a proud name."

"Jefferson is a slave name."

"Who tell you that?"

"Mom, it's in books. History books. Library books."

"Is that what they learning you now? And don't be rolling up your big eyes at me."

"Mom, blacks in the States used to name their children after presidents. For luck or something. They're still doing it. They've got Andrew Jacksons, Jefferson Johnsons, and George Washingtons, all over the place."

Shirley bites her lip but can't stop herself from snapping, "Boy, is your own father gave you that name. Is a proud name. Is a good name. But nothing is good enough for you now."

"Can I go now?" Sad Eyes stares her down.

"Go to the garage; George wants to talk to you. And make sure you find your tail back here before the eleven o'clock news!"

The kitchen screen door flaps in her face.

~

"Mom says you want to talk to me?"

George puts his beer down on his stack of newspapers and stares Sad Eyes up and down. George is a huge, imposing man who knows how to use his size to intimidate; he glares down at Sad Eyes, who remains cautious yet nonchalant, near the garage door, like a stray dog ready to hightail it in a split-second.

"Your mammy don't want you smoking," George breaks the impasse with a long swallow of beer. "Especially in the house. You got that? It's a nasty habit. Bad for you."

George tries a softer tack, "How you expect to make the basketball team when school start back—"

"—I done with that."

"Is so?"

"Yeah."

"So, all the practice you been practicing all summer is just for so?"

Sad Eyes looks away but recovers in a flash, "Can I go now?"

George casts another long stare at Sad Eyes but he can't reel him in. "Where you headed? By Verna?"

"Yeah," Sad Eyes wheels his bike out of the garage.

"Her mammy still working afternoons?"

George's grin follows his furious pedaling out the driveway and down the street. Why do they always have to grin like they know your business? Sad Eyes rears his Chopper into a wheelie that he sustains for a full block for the benefit of a knot of neighbourhood kids.

~

"Boy, it eh have no Rastamen in Red Deer," Verna says.

Sad Eyes is as quiet as a mouse, while Verna parts and divides his hair into sections.

"Let me see, let me see," Denise jumps in, "that rat-tail comb eh go work." She studies Sad Eyes's head from all angles. "Eh-eh, that just don't look right."

"Don't worry with she," Verna mocks a stab at Denise with the comb. "What she know 'bout hairdressing? She well bold. Girl, keep your two cents to yourself."

Sad Eyes watches his medium-sized Afro diminish into small braids, not what he was expecting at all, garden worms instead of jungle snakes.

"You look so cute. Doesn't he look cute?" Verna steps back to admire her handiwork.

Sad Eyes confronts the mirror; what he sees is all too neat and orderly, like his mother's backyard garden.

"I want dreadlocks, just a few long fat locks."

"You don't have enough hair for that yet," Verna says. "Cornrow is the style for you now, Jeffery."

"When your hair grows long enough," Verna comforts him, "I'll braid this section together into one, and this one into these two here, and one or maybe even two down the middle." Verna trails her fingernails down the neat pathways she's designed on his scalp, sculpting it out for his imagination.

Verna lightly rakes her nails up and down his neck. When she gets an immediate rise from his fifteen-year-old flesh, she gives a satisfied giggle and joins Denise sorting through the pile of CDs by the stereo.

"—Not Reggae Rhythms," Denise heads her off. "By the time we make the concert in Edmonton tomorrow, they'll be so stale."

"Play some other reggae," Sad Eyes offers up in compromise.

"Okay," Denise and Verna agree. "Anything but Bob Marley."

"What!" Sad Eyes takes up an astounded stance. "Marley is the prophet! Play *Catch a Fire*."

The three-way argument takes on fresh fuel.

~

"What you looking for trouble for?" George calls out from the TV room.

Shirley is going through Jeffrey's room; she is perplexed by what she finds. Picture books on Africa? And Jamaica? Some of them long overdue from the library. Some photocopied articles on Rastafarians, some on Haile Selassie, some on the Coptic faith. She calls on George for help; he refuses to leave the TV.

"George, this evening when you talked to him? What'd he say?"

"I told him you don't like him smoking, and for him not to do it in the house."

"Nothing else?"

"He was heading off to Verna's."

"That is another thing that have me worried. Verna's mother does work too much afternoons; it not right to leave a young girl like that home alone. It not right for Jeff to spend so much time over there. If you ask me."

"I don't think anything going on." George leans as far back as his La-Z-Boy allows, settling himself in for a long evening. He converts a M.A.S.H. rerun into news.

Shirley plumps herself down on the sofa with her basket of crocheting. "Not yet, not yet, but it bound to happen." She adds a line to her crocheting, "You can't leave two teenagers alone by themselves. When Verna belly swell, who you think she mother go come cursing and bawling to, eh? Who you think she go blame? Is me. Is my name she go scandalize."

George knows that no matter how much he twists and turns, there is no way to avoid it; Shirley and her crochet needle will be a thorn in his side all night. He searches around the dial with the remote control; he kneads the sour gas rumblings in his belly until it forms the lump of a question; Shirley, why don't we pack up?

Why don't we leave this place and go back home? He leaves for a fresh beer during a commercial and returns with it unspoken.

~

At midnight, Red Deer reveals itself: the hood ornament on a semi outside a neon-lit diner; a brass belt-buckle holding up some cowboy's dreams; the stasis point between Edmonton and Calgary where AM stations rival it out for the abortion and adultery music crowd. What does a fifteen-year-old black boy, twice uprooted, now replanted in Red Deer, wish for when he sees a falling star?

Hello Africa! Check it out!

He is racing along a narrow pathway through the jungle; he must take to the air, leaping to avoid quicksand, alligators, a herd of rhinos, and a pack of nipping jackals in turn. A construction site becomes the deserted ruin of a vanished civilization. He has a message for the Emperor's eyes only. He must not fail. The fate of the entire Sahara campaign is in his hands ... spies are everywhere. He weaves left then right, cresting the final rise; the hidden city is below, chains of light marking its borders. Now is not the time to stop and admire its beauty; he may already be too late, is his fear, and as he dismounts, fantasy and reality collide in a clatter in the garage.

George has sunk into his La-Z-Boy, disappeared into sleep. Shirley plucks the remote control from his outstretched hand and clucks through the National followed by local news, then she clicks to the American stations to watch most of the same footage.

News hour is Shirley's favourite time of day. George is

almost always asnooze; his snores add the perfect tonal antidote to the nightly images of a collapsing world. She can hiss her dismay and suck her teeth in disgust at each act of terror; every natural disaster is confirmation of her belief in the biblical fury of Armageddon. It's bound to happen, and soon; in her cosmology, even George and those like him who look for oil and gas are leeches sucking the earth dry.

Some years back, when the Yankee and them went and invade even little Grenada, eh-eh, that was her turning point. There is no place on this earth that truly safe again. Her house is her retreat. In her church where she knows every hymn by heart she will stand. Red Deer is her high ground.

The local news on the American superstation is winding down; it's almost 12:30. Where is he? Where is that blasted boy? Her boiling anger is quickly swallowed in a wash of guilt and fear. If only he was hiding some Playboy magazines, she could still vex, but at least she could deal with that. But this business about Coptics? And Rastamen? All of that Jamaican nonsense had come to Trinidad after Independence. But all of that was left behind once they came to Canada. How he could be mess up in that Rasta business quite here in Red Deer?

Sad Eyes tries a quick finesse through the kitchen past the TV room and up the stairs, but his mom calls him back.

"Didn't I tell you to be back before the news finish?"

"Sorry," he mumbles from halfway up the stairs.

"Come here, Mister man. Who you think you talking to? Who—"

Shirley has the TV remote control in one hand, and her crochet needle in the other. The hand with the crochet needle rises, then freezes, in midair; then the needle begins to quiver and move on its own like a divining rod, drawing Shirley along. Sad Eyes feints and runs past her down the stairs, he backpedals, until he's cornered in the kitchen.

"How you could do me this?" Shirley hisses.

"How you could do me this?" Shirley's hiss turns to steam.

Sad Eyes stands his ground.

"Not in my house. You don't come and play Rastaman. With the drugs and all that sort of nastiness nonsense. Not in my focking house."

He has never, in his entire life, ever heard his mom swear. When she raises the crochet needle, it's his turn to scream, "Oh God, no mammy! No!"

"What you calling God for? Who God you calling? You calling your nasty Rastaman God? You think he go come and save you? Not in my house!"

George comes lumbering into the kitchen; his sleepy red eyes open wide in surprise.

"Shirley!" He takes one giant step towards her and grabs her hand with the needle.

"Let it go. Let it go," George says until the needle clatters to the kitchen floor.

Sad Eyes bolts past them, up the stairs to his room.

～

"Let it leave until morning," George tries his best to calm her down.

Shirley couldn't, wouldn't leave it at that.

She sets up camp outside Sad Eyes's bedroom door with her bible and her rosary, and starts to pray.

Long and loud, she rains hail and holy Mary's down on his door, but every so often her prayers would dry up and she would issue threats instead.

"You grounded for life. Next step is reform school. You playing Rastaman? Bet I make you go out there and catch arse and get a job. You think is work I working to support your nasty Rastaman vices?

"You sleeping?" She rattles his door. "You sleeping? Bet I come in there an cut off every last one of those picky-plaits you sporting?"

Around three o'clock, Shirley starts weaving her prayers and threats into a litany of all the sacrifices she has made on his behalf.

"Who shit you out into this world? Who wiped your arse? When your daddy come an drop down dead, who bring you Canada? Who buy you that bike? Who put clothes on your back? Food in your belly?"

Who, who, who … her pitch gets higher and hotter, until it becomes white noise, one long sustained laser of a moan that cuts through his door. But it never reaches Sad Eyes; he is safe in the Emperor's palace.

He is exalted to a high position at the Emperor's right hand, and the entire palace is decorated for a festival in his honour. Warriors tell the deeds of his great courage and bravery—how he, single-handedly, withstood the enemy under tremendous fire, how he escaped and saved the entire Sahara campaign. The Emperor himself rises to speak, and with one gesture, the banquet hall is silenced: "And how shall we reward this great warrior? What will we call this great warrior? We must give you a new name."

The Emperor sits back down to ponder. "We need a sign. We hereby declare that when your locks are full-grown, you will have your new name."

Sad Eyes takes his fantasies safe into his dreams.

~

"You're grounded!" Verna yells into the phone at him. "The concert is tonight. How she could ground you?"

"She don't like my new hairstyle," Sad Eyes says.

Verna relays this to Denise.

"What I tell you yesterday? You see you see," Denise gloats.

"But we have tickets and all," Verna sighs into the phone.

"I'm still going," Sad Eyes says.

"Are you crazy?" Verna shrieks at him.

"What she could do? Ground me again? Reground me? I done grounded for life already."

"Boy, I don't want your mammy vex with me, next thing she phone my mammy and is grounded I grounded too."

"They can't keep track;" Sad Eyes grows bolder by the minute, "both of them have to work."

"Is true, is true," Verna is willing to be convinced for the sake of the concert.

Denise and Verna chatter back and forth. Sad Eyes cuts them off. "Two o'clock sharp, at the bus station," he hangs up.

And starts packing his suitcase.

~

"Oh my God, oi!" Shirley is on the verge. "Find him for me. You go find him for me, please God."

The young policeman makes some more scribbles in his notebook: DD, RY (domestic dispute, runaway youth). He proceeds in textbook fashion; separate the parents, and always give one of them something useful to do.

"Can you tell us if he took a coat? And find a recent photo?"

"Yes, yes," Shirley runs to check.

"Can you tell me anything about the two girls?" The policeman earnestly searches George's face. "Which one, is your, um, stepson, closer to?"

The reference to stepson puts George off balance; how do they find these things out so quickly, he wonders? "Verna."

"Is she um, pregnant?"

George meets and holds the young policeman's gaze. "No, I don't think so."

"But you're not sure?"

"No," George can't make up his mind, "I'm not sure." He decides to level with the cop. "Jeff and his mom had a big row, the day before yesterday."

"How big a, um, row?" The policeman asks. "Was there any, um, physical violence?"

"No," George hesitates. "It didn't come to that."

"How, um, close did it come?"

The policeman angles towards the door. "Normally we have to wait 48 hours from the time of a report before declaring a person officially missing, but I'll get this in right away to the

RCMP. They'll pass it on to the Edmonton Police. We'll do everything we can."

George follows the policeman outside. "Is there anything I can do?"

The policeman gives George a checklist. "Take a good look around the house and let us know if any money or anything valuable is missing. Chances are he'll cool down and it'll blow over once he realizes he's broke and hungry. If he turns up on the drag, he'll be easy enough to spot."

"I'm going up to Edmonton to look for him," George says. "Any ideas as to where I should start?"

"Downtown. The drag between 95th and 97th. And there's a, um, queer stroll at the top of Bellamy Hill." The cop shrugs as he folds himself into his cruiser and pulls away.

George can feel the peeping eyes of his neighbours. He wants to yell, Mind your own blasted business, and he wants to cry, Why you don't come and help? Come and at least make the offer. Instead, he slams the door and goes inside to take this argument up with Shirley. People back home don't live like this. How people could live so? Shirley has no strength left to fight with him. She sits at her kitchen table trying to rock away the gnawing pain growing in her belly.

~

"Jeffery, come go. Come and go back with us nah boy."

Sad Eyes doesn't even bother to answer Verna; he's wishing he'd ordered a pop or at least some hot chocolate instead of this bitter cup of coffee. Of course Verna and Denise had to pig out before they could get on the bus back to Red Deer, and they expect him to pay. Look at them, wolfing down a burger each, with large fries and onion rings too! He adds this latest extravagance and subtracts it from what is left in his wallet. The few remaining notes look so thin and lonely in there.

As they leave the A&W and head towards the bus terminal, a place to stay is his major worry. Verna and Denise are still in a swoon; they recreate the concert and give two-part harmony renditions of all the hits.

At the bus station, he stows his suitcase in a locker.

"Come on Jeffery, let's go back home," Verna pleads with him. "We're in enough shit already. Your mammy bound to vex, but as you yourself say, what can she do?"

Verna runs her hand up the back of his shirt and massages his neck, but Sad Eyes pulls away before she scratches away his resolve.

"Leave him, leave him," Denise sniffs. "He playing man, come come, leave him. Let him be a mule."

Exhilaration and fear are close cousins; they take over from Verna and Denise and dog his every step as he exits the bus terminal.

~

Beaver Hill Park is a lumpy, manmade oasis, downtown, off Jasper on Fifth. At night, it is a magnet that pulls the street people in for rest stops between tricks, where deals are fixed or come unglued, with cops, cons, the curious, and the lost.

"Yo! Hey Yo! Hold up, hold up there nah man."

Sad Eyes puts his feet on standby alert.

"What wrong with you? You playing deaf an' dumb? Is you I calling, you. Yes you."

Sad Eyes is speechless; he can't help but stare.

"Something lose with you, or what? You have a name? Or you lose that too?"

Check him out! A Rastaman! A real live Rastaman! Look at those dreadlocks! Check it out! Down past his waist.

"Where you from? I don't see you 'round here before." The Rastaman catches up to him, "Where you from, brother?"

Sad Eyes swallows his excitement; the Emperor must have sent him. "Red Deer."

"Red Deer? Red Deer tuh rass. I man na' know it have locksmen in Red Deer."

Sad Eyes makes a close-up inspection of his first in-the-flesh Rastaman. He is dying to blurt out his surprise; his Rasta is not even black—not very. He's what his mom calls a 'Douglar', he looks mostly East Indian, thin and wiry, wearing a T-shirt printed with the Ethiopian flag under green army surplus fatigues—and jewelry, lots of jewelry. His beard is still straggling in under a big beak of a nose. Sad Eyes relaxes as he realizes this Rasta can't be much older than himself.

"They call me The Saint," the Rasta says. "From Toussaint."

Sad Eyes looks him over.

"My real name is Sunil Mohammed, but when I turn Ras, I take on Toussaint. You ever hear 'bout Toussaint? Toussaint L'Ouverture?"

Sad Eyes shakes his head, "No."

"It have Rasta who does go all the way back to Africa to get name. Not me. Long before them African an' them wake up to

Independence, Toussaint done gone and overthrow the French and them in Haiti. The Emperor Napoleon send he own brother-in-law self to fight Toussaint. Is only treachery and jealousy what cause Toussaint to fall into exile and die. And is Toussaint who curse Napoleon and make him lose. You know 'bout that? You think I lie? Go an read for yourself; look up how Toussaint end up, then look what happen in the end to Nappy. He come an dead in exile on the isle of Elba.

"Toussaint say tell Nappy 'Whatever you do to me, I go do worse for you.'

"Is Toussaint who call down the jes grew to free up his people in Haiti. Yes. Is Toussaint who let it loose. The white people an them eh stupid, since then, they cut Haiti off, clean clean. They say it have Voodoo an Zombie an all kinda thing down there. Even to this day they saying so. How Haiti this and Haiti that. Now they saying how is AIDS an all that nastiness what come from Haiti. Don't fall for that. Is the jes grew, in they tail. Jes grew!"

Sad Eyes picks up the chant. "Jes grew? Jes grew!"

"After famine flood and fire, Africa will rise." The Saint prophesizes. "They have the famine now. Soon is the flood, and look South Africa and tell me if you don't see smoke. All Africa children must get ready to go back home now!"

The Saint has plenty more to spout. Sad Eyes sits entranced, eager as a sponge, soaking it all in without discrimination, until his new fount suddenly dries up. "The Man is on the prowl and I'm holding. You holding? We better cut from here."

Sad Eyes and The Saint abandon the cool darkness of the park and for an instant they are innocent children again, pure speed, accelerating past the extravagantly lit showrooms of car dealerships along Jasper. Sneakers criss-cross in alleys where shadows take substance from a late summer's night, and the faint strains of childhood games of police and thief touch now on real siren nerves.

~

George doesn't know where next to turn and look.

The police had already pegged and pulled him over for a quiz. Their advice was for him to haul his tail back to Red Deer and leave this business with them. The same car circling and circling on the drag was bound to attract some other attention. Yet another one of the working girls approaches George.

"Honey, what you looking for?"

"A fifteen-year-old black boy," George says.

"Honey," she says, "I can be anything you want. But for that you're going to have to close your eyes real tight and wish real hard."

"Hop in," George reaches for his wallet. "Maybe we could do some business."

What would Shirley do if she could see me now? George can't help but chuckle as he looks at his passenger. The hooker is taking advantage of the warm car to massage her feet. Her bare legs are two extra-long distractions. George tries to explain about Jeffery and he finds himself opening up about his troubles. He tries to describe the sour gas feeling in his stomach; she nods in all the right places.

"Everybody wants to go back," she says. "I hear that all the time."

"This is a little bit of a switch for me," she smiles. "Most of the time all my clients really want is just someone to talk to, but after. They all feel I'm Petro Canada; you know, they've got to pump their money's worth first."

George chuckles, "What do you tell them? About going back?"

"There's no easy answer to that," she says. "Go back and take a good look. But don't you go confusing a holiday with a look."

George nods to her wisdom.

"If you want," she smiles, "now that the talking's over, we could go to a little place I know. Room service. Good rates."

George laughs, no, he'll keep on looking.

"Suit yourself, but Saturday is my busy night so let me out on my corner. I'll ask around. If I hear anything, I'll flag you."

"Thanks," says George.

He resumes his search, on foot now, crawling through the human wreckage on 95th. In and out of every bar, back to Jasper, up to 109th.

~

For a big city, George thinks, this place well dead on a Sunday. He decides to make one last swing through downtown before cashing in and heading back to Red Deer. It's the kind of Sunday that reminds him of back home, hot hot, blue skies, lazy white clouds in no hurry at all. This sort of Sunday is for the beach, with a big pot of peas and rice and enough ice for the grog, food, family, friends. For the amount of people that live here in Edmonton, nothing is open downtown, nothing except: the library!

F.B. ANDRÉ

~

George spots him easily enough, up on the second floor, stacked up in periodicals with a big Atlas of Africa and some books on Napoleon. George stalks him quietly, until he's able to slide into the seat right next to Sad Eyes.

Sad Eyes looks up. George sees the flash of relief and confusion, before Sad Eyes can put on his *hardened* look.

"Is Napoleon now? Eh-eh, and Toussaint?"

Sad Eyes looks at George, surprised.

"Toussaint was way ahead of his time, man," George smiles. "He had General Le Clerc and even Napoleon himself well worried up."

Sad Eyes looks even more surprised at George.

"Toussaint, Marcus Garvey, even Stokley Carmichael," George presses in his wedge. "Down through the years, a lot of the big black leaders come from the West Indies, you know that? You make a study of all the big black movements in the States or over in England, and time after time you go see how some West Indians always near the centre, always providing the backbone and the brainpower."

George turns to the Atlas and devotes himself to the topography of Africa; he lets Sad Eyes brew for a minute.

"These maps don't tell you a blasted thing. Where Mandinga? Where Bemba? And Shambaa? Where is Timbuktu?"

"Timbuktu is a real place?" Sad Eyes perks up.

"How you mean?" George is taken aback. "I bet you hear all about Athens and Rome, eh? Well it had a time when Timbuktu outshine all of them. It was the seat of learning for the world. It

126

had one of the first universities ever, one of the best libraries."

Sad Eyes looks at George with new respect.

"What is jes grew?" He asks. "Do you know about jes grew?"

George checks over his left shoulder twice, then swivels and scans around the library, as if to make sure no one can overhear. He gets up and pushes his chair neatly up to the table. "I man saw Hailie Selassie when he come down to Trinidad."

"The Emperor?" Sad Eyes asks.

"The son of Solomon." George takes a step away. "The Conquering Lion of the tribe of Judah.

"Selassie went Jamaica first," George casts his bait. "Rastas were waiting for him at the airport, by the thousands. Them Rastas believe Selassie is God on earth," George starts to move away, then stops, "but when he landed in Trinidad, man, it was a different story."

George knows when he has a bite; he walks away in measured steps. He hears the squeak of Sad Eyes's chair.

"Jes grew was rampant. Independence was still fresh. People lined both sides of the road, clapping and dancing. The government handed out little Ethiopia and little Trinidad and Tobago flags.

"You ever hear the name Kilhany Goathead?"

"No." Sad Eyes is all ears.

"Kilhany Goathead was the spitting image of Hailie Selassie. Kilhany Goathead was well-known about the place. A rum jumbie. Kilhany Goathead was a man who was infested with the jes grew. When that motorcade, with Selassie standing up and waving in a big limousine, reach the bypass coming into San Fernando, somebody in the crowd pointed and shouted at the Emperor, 'Look, Kilhany Goathead!'

"Then the jes grew broke loose. The jes grew took over. People started to laugh. People laughed so hard they had to sit down; people laughed so hard they were falling down with laughing.

"Emperor Selassie didn't know what all to think. Selassie just come from Jamaica, where thousands flocked to see him, praising and calling him God. And look here, people laughing so hard, they peeing themselves."

"No!" Sad Eyes is securely hooked. All that's left for George to do is to tow him outside.

"What happened then?" Sad Eyes runs to catch up with George, "What is jes grew? What?"

"Take it easy man," George opens the car door. "Is a good hour-and-a-half pull back to Red Deer. Come, you ready?"

George doesn't wait for the silence to grow; he interprets Sad Eyes's first blink.

"Come, Jeff. Come let we go home."

ANOTHER WORLD

"CAN YOU COME out and talk to Hoover?"

That was the booming voice of Hoover's cousin, Big Gemma, the one he's staying by, on the phone.

"Hoover talks about you all the time," she says, her voice rising with the lie. "He's not working these days ... at all." She trails off.

They live out past Clareview, after where the LRT ends, then another ten or twelve blocks, in what, if this were the States, they'd call a Project. Up here it's sanitized, subsidized housing—three small cubes on top of two squares, postage-stamp (from a tiny country) front lawn, two scarecrow stickman trees—exact and faithful replicas from the architect's blueprints. Theirs is the second house from the dead-end, where a half-erected noise fence is drawn across in front of the railway tracks like a curtain that's missing hooks and already needs a washing and an ironing.

It's well past noon by the time I get out there. Getting up into the heat of the day. It's early August, but there's that feel of Fall about the mornings already—although by now the sun has found its resolve and the ants' nest of kids playing on the lawn have good reason to squeal and squabble over the length of garden hose.

I count eight—make it nine-kids, all under seven or so, all different colours and shades like in a soft-drink commercial, except this one boy a-head-and-a-half-taller. He looks to be in the throes of puberty, gangly, all arms and legs. He and Deeann, Big Gemma's daughter, race inside. Deeann is two-and-a-half-years of terror; she comes back twirled around Gemma's considerable calf. Gemma shakes her loose, steadies her drink, and blinks me inside.

"Deeann, go and call Hoover. Go and call Hoover. Go tell Hoover somebody's here to see him. Go on. Call Hoover. Deeann."

Deeann's about as high as a footstool and as hard as a Frisbee; she goes bouncing up the steps.

In the living room, a sofa and a settee come together in an L. A massive TV straddles the hypotenuse, a turned-on Cyclops muttering just below hearing. The rest of the room is boxes and boxes piled high. Magazines are stuck and buttered between winter coats; rolled-up tubes of carpet are precariously balanced against a hat rack.

"Moving?"

"How'd you guess?" Gemma deadpans.

I get the settee. Gemma's on the sofa with a friend of hers that I met once before but can't remember the name of. She ups and claims three of the kids outside as hers. Another woman comes out from behind a wall of boxes, from where the kitchen must be, holding a tiny baby against her hip and testing a bottle by jerking a few drops against the crook of her forearm.

She looks a lot younger than Gemma and her friend at first, but only because she's almost thin. She has that kind of skin that's patchy but smooth. She eases down besides me on the settee. I stare and make faces at her baby.

"Hoover! Hoover!" Gemma shouts up the stairwell.

"Hoover's sleepin'," Deeann comes marching back down.

"That boy," Gemma says, "he don't get up afore two o'clock now. He don't get up afore two o'clock no more. That's when his show comes on. He don't get up afore that now."

"He still wearing the black?" giggles Gemma's friend whose name I can't recall.

"Yes child," says Gemma. "He wearing the black for Gatlin." She laughs that "teehee teehee" laugh that some fat women have.

I don't know what they're going on about and I must look it. Gemma's other friend, the one with the patchy skin, says by way of explaining, "Gatlin's dead. He went down in a plane crash. Up over BC. He was doing some big business deal."

"They never yet find the body," says Gemma.

"He mightn't even be dead," says the friend who I met before. "They could reincarnate him with a different face and a different body if they want." The friend continues. "It all depends on the money. If he's too greedy—they'll just leave his arse in the forests up in BC."

Gemma leads a round of nodding. "Hoover's wearing the black. Since then Hoover's only wearing the black."

My face must still have that fresh-from-Mars look. Gemma and her friends start with the teehee teeheeing again.

Gemma fans her hand across her mouth, then she waves the wine bottle around, then she makes as if to get up, then she shouts, "Hoover! Hoover!"

"Deeann, Deeann," Gemma says, "go and call Hoover. Call Hoover."

Hoover's from back east. East east—New Brunswick. When

you ask him and Big Gemma, ask any of that crowd where, they'll tell you Moncton. Ask again and you'll get a list of small towns nobody outside of being born there ever heard of, and everyone is a fini-cousin related by in-laws more than by blood. The law says it's safe enough for them to get married up and breed if they want.

Gemma and Hoover are family more than most by circumstances—the main circumstance being they're from the same one-blink of a town and did their growing up together. They came out west about the same time. And when hard times caught up, "It's only natural," as Big Gemma says, "that we end up living like family."

"My husband Clyde," she says, "he don't mind the extra mouth. But now seeing as he's out of work himself... he still don't blame Hoover for nothing, mind you, but he's mighty testy now," she says. She sees "a trouble coming, sure as rain. Sure as rain."

The other women nod with Gemma. Upstairs the toilet flushes and sends a shiver through the house. Deeann revs at the foot of the stairs. Gemma swivels and waves the big bottle of Brights' Sparkling Red house wine around in a question with a foregone answer. Her two friends reach for their share of communion. I cradle my beer. The gangly kid comes skipping down the stairs.

"Boy, you been in that washroom all this time? What you been doing in there all this time?" Gemma and her friends laugh.

The kid freezes, then backs up the steps like in an instant replay, "Nuttin'!" he says.

Gemma and her friends cackle. The boy darts forward out the door.

"That's Ralph and Barbara's boy," Gemma says. "Barbara's gonna have her hands full this next while."

"He's a cutie," says the one next to me on the settee. "He's going to be some handsome when he fills out."

"And you gonna make sure and be there when he does," says the other friend. "Girl, you're a cradle-robber."

Gemma cackles, then sends Deeann on a mission, "You tell that Hoover his friend Ray is here to see him. You tell his majesty to haul his tail out of bed. Right now!" Deeann goes spinning off like a top.

"Gemma," says her friend, the one with the patchy skin, next to me, "you shouldn't teach her to say things like that—"

"—Child," Gemma slices, "mind your own business, yes. She is my child. She have to live in this world."

Her friend next to me makes her mouth into an O as if she is willing to argue the point, but changes her mind and coos to her baby instead. We can hear Deeann shrill away at Hoover, then she comes stamping down the stairs, one at a time. "He up now," Deeann pronounces. And we can hear water running.

"Good," says Gemma. "You go back outside and play. You tell them to watch it with that hose, eh. I don't want you all tracking mud in here. You hear me?"

Deeann is already out the door, her screams joining those of the other kids in a third-world symphony. The big boy has control of the garden hose and is conducting with its stream; some of the smaller kids don't have sense enough to close their eyes and stop screaming when he trains the water on them, they fall to the ground blinking and sputtering. Gemma has to go over to the door and give him a hard look of warning.

Hoover comes yawning down the stairs. He's six foot one inch tall and under one-fifty. His hair is pulled back tight into four fat braids, and his sparse beard looks like people who ran for but missed the bus. The blue in his denim jeans is almost all gone, and you can count his ribs sticking out under his black T-shirt, one by one.

"Say-hey! Ray!" His headlights come on for an instant, "You two bitches here again?" he shakes his head at Gemma's girl-friends. "Brr," he growls at the patchy-skin one next to me, cup-ping his hands protectively over his crotch, he grins, "Not today Carol," he groans, "I—I just can't."

"You never could," she shoots right back at him.

Hoover doubles over and expels all the air from his lungs pretending as if he's been hit by a bolo punch. He laughs as he limps offstage into the kitchen.

"Say! You ready for another beer Ray?"

"You're pretty free 'n easy with what ain't yours," Gemma chimes from the sofa.

"I'm okay," I say as quick as I can.

Gemma tries to sidestep a bit, "Ain't mine neither. It's between you and Clyde."

Hoover comes out of the kitchen with one beer and hands it over to me.

"Move over," he squeezes in besides Carol on the settee. "Maybe Carol here'll give me some of her milk. If her baby don't drink it. If that don't belong to Clyde too." He flashes Gemma a long look. Gemma chooses to ignore it.

This is the Carol I'd heard tell about before from Hoover. How she come out from down east, must've been a little less than a year ago, with her man. And how he kept on going. It's not clear if she got pregnant before or after he left. But, I do remember Hoover telling how she sure took a lot of consoling after he was gone. I take another closer look at her baby. It's still too soon to tell who, if anyone, the baby looks like.

Hoover keeps his stare fixed on Gemma. I'm wondering why she doesn't even try to shoo him away. Then I look over at Hoover; his spine is too straight and he's inclined forward ever so slightly, hands crossed on his knees. His eyes aren't on Gemma anymore. My guess is he's gone; he's bored through her, through the walls, and the last house on the block, down past the half-finished noise curtain and out across the tracks.

Hoover's gone. Long distance. New area code.

Gemma and her friends fidget; they all look someplace else.

Outside, the string-band of soaked kids yell and shiver at a passing rain cloud. Inside, Gemma moves around on the sofa, unsticking herself as she tries to find a fresh cool spot. One of the little kids comes running inside crying for her mama. Deeann tags after her.

"What happen? Deeann?" Gemma welcomes the interruption.

Big Gemma to the rescue, she gets up and goes outside to lead the inquisition personally. The whole neighbourhood can hear her ranting; her finale is to chase the big kid away. By the time she comes back inside, she's sweating freely from the heat. Her friend over on the sofa fills up her glass for her; Gemma takes the glass and the bottle. Her friend goes back to trying to hush-hush her little one. "Don't cry, Do-do, don't cry," she sings over and over.

Hoover starts sipping on the beer he had handed me; now he's smiling and making faces for Carol's baby. Carol divides her attention between the baby and me. I catch a wink from Hoover. The cloud refuses to blow over.

The band of kids come rushing up the front steps all at once, led by Deeann, "My daddy's comin', my daddy's comin'." Then they turn as one and race to the sidewalk.

Clyde is a handsome man. Gemma takes a lot of pride in that; she tugs and straightens her housecoat before going over to blockade the door.

Clyde comes in towing a case of beer and a friend. His friend is a squat, powerful man who has that I've-been-out-of-work-too-long look, rock turning to Jell-O. Clyde nods at me and glares at Hoover.

Clyde tests me with his handshake, grunts me a pass.

"You shit your bed?" Clyde goes straight after Hoover, "You crap yourself? No other reason for you to be up so early."

Clyde makes a show of consulting his watch. "Your show ain't on for half-hour."

Clyde laughs along with his friend.

Hoover sits stiff and formal like a praying mantis on the edge of the settee. I notice Carol edge away. Deeann is twined around Clyde's legs, insistent. Clyde hoists her above his head and swings her back and forth; she screams with delight.

You can smell that Clyde's in a real good mood. Gemma smells it too; she intercepts Deeann on the next fly pass.

"Lennox and me—we sold my car," Clyde looks to Lennox for confirmation.

"Got twelve bills for it," he looks to Gemma for approval.

She can't hide her disappointment.

"Shoot, sheet, shit," Clyde says, waving his beer as he conjugates. Gemma's way ahead of him with addition and subtraction; it's a long ways yet until the next check. She plants her left hand on her hip and holds out the right.

Clyde reaches into his pocket and hands Gemma a ball of money.

Gemma makes a fist; anyone can see her pressure's rising. "How're we gonna move now?" It comes out of her in a hoarse whisper.

"No problem," says Clyde, "we've still got the car until Friday when the guy can come up with the rest. Meantime, we have a down payment from him, not so Lennox? Not so?"

"Yes yes," Lennox nods.

Gemma looks from one to the other, tightening up on the ball of money.

"I have the keys," Clyde's been saving his trump for last. He jangles them, "They say we can move in anytime."

Gemma tugs her housecoat together and does a slow 360 turn, graceful, just like that. Her two girlfriends dance towards her but she reaches out for her Clyde first. He buckles. Big Gemma is quite a handful.

"Let's go over right now," Gemma is excited. "Let's go and see what sort of state they left the place in. We'll march in with a mop and pail."

"Sure," says Clyde. "You go up and change. As soon as you ready. Once me and Lennox finish up these beers, we ready."

"Ray," Hoover calls me over. He had quietly eased his way out of the frame to the front steps. The kids are into obstacle races, starting three lawns over and ending down at the dead end.

Clyde and Lennox come outside with fresh beers; Clyde asks if I'm working. I nod and he says how he's glad to see at least some people still have a job.

He and Lennox talk about "the depression they keep callin' recession." We amble down to his car and mine and sniff around them both. I allow that the guy he's selling to got himself one hell of a good deal. Then I take some of the sour out of selling for Clyde; "Seeing as how," I say, "you sure got your money's worth first."

"Yes yes. Yes man," Lennox agrees with me.

Hoover sits on the hood of my car, as still as the ornament. He's looking away down the street, across the tracks.

Deeann runs up and soaks Clyde with the hose; he wrestles it from her and gives all the kids a good soaking. Then he turns it on Hoover.

Hoover sits like stone. Clyde bends the hose near the spout to let the pressure build, then strafes Hoover again. Hoover finally hops off the car and goes and stands in the middle of the road, out of range. Clyde keeps the pressure up on the hose; whenever Hoover takes a step back towards the car, Clyde lets him have it. Both of them are dead serious.

Carol and her baby and Gemma's other friend come outside and watch from the front steps. Carol's baby gives off a thin yelp. I can see Big Gemma outlined behind the curtains upstairs.

Hoover stays, swaying arms folded across his chest, out of range. Clyde turns the hose back over to Deeann. The sun comes back out again. It's hot. As hot as August ever gets.

Big Gemma comes out ready to go. They angle in the mop first, then she and her friends bundle into the back seat. Lennox is up front with Clyde. Deeann clamours and gets to go. Gemma's friend instructs Hoover to keep an eye on her brood. Hoover nods from the middle of the street. When Clyde goes down to the dead end to make the U-turn, Hoover comes back over to the sidewalk.

Hoover gets two beers out of the fridge. We sit on the front steps and watch the kids. They're lining up, begging to be sprayed now; the water seems to dry almost as fast as it hits the concrete.

We talk. A bit about old times. Then I talk about my job for a while. I ask, Had any luck? Have you tried? Not even part-time? Been looking? How about? I get a lot of sideways nods.

"Say—Ray," Hoover asks, "what time's it?"

"Just coming on two o'clock," I say.

Hoover bounces up, slaps the seat of his jeans, and goes inside. He changes the channel and sets the volume to suit himself, then settles on the sofa, spine straight; he's leaning forward ever so slightly. The theme music comes on first, then the voice-over… "And now for the continuing story of *Another World.*"

"It's too blame hot to be inside watching TV, Hoover." I try and coax him out.

Hoover drinks from his beer with a slow-motion machine movement.

"What say we head downtown to the Cecil? The Kingsway?" Hoover barely shakes his head, "No."

His park lights are on.

The kids escort me to my car. I go down to the dead-end and

make the turn. I drive past the house, slow. Up ahead the asphalt shivers where the heat horizon is, playing tricks with my eyes. When it's bright like this outside, you can't make out a thing inside.

I'VE DONE TWO rooms so far, the kitchen and my old bedroom. I've spent the entire morning listening to a soundtrack of old things tearing; I've been packing up and throwing away bits of my childhood, and out of a duty that comes with being the eldest, bagging into polyurethane lumps what's left of my mother's marriage, her life and our times in Fort McMurray.

My mother always said that one day she would get as far away from the Fort as humanly possible. Eighteen months ago my youngest brother quit Syncrude and left the Fort. He was the last one left at home. My mother rented out her house and took a one-year contract, doing what she's always been doing, Community Health Nurse. But on the other side of the earth. In Papua New Guinea.

Six months ago my mother phoned in the middle of the night. She got her contract extended for two more years.

"Sell," my mother said.

"List it with Miriam Wallace," my mother instructed.

"Miriam always said, 'If ever, whenever you're ready,' so give her the listing."

I was surprised when Miriam called with an offer. And shocked at how little.

Telephone conversations from Papua New Guinea are umbilical miracles. My mother's voice said, "Take it: Miriam knows what she's doing." No further questions.

"You go up and tidy things up, Hazel." It was definitely her voice, flattened out, coming from all the way around the world inside my head. No inflections, no hints, not a clue on what she wants to keep or share, or throw out.

~

Roberta and I were best friends all through school. We sat together from grade five until halfway through grade twelve, when Roberta had to drop out. We shared everything, including the feeling that we were "psychic sisters." A part of our special bond was that we even had the same last name—Jenkings. Even after my mother separated and then went back to using her maiden name after the divorce, I still feel that she, we, I am a Jenkings.

I still can't think of my mother as a Miss Henderson or as a Ms. Anything. I've settled on using just her maiden name without title or adornment, Helena Henderson, when I write or forward her correspondence to Papua New Guinea. And now I can't hardly think of Roberta as anything other than Mrs. Kennard Ferguson.

We've always kept in touch. Roberta does most of the writing and when I get to feeling guilty about not answering, I phone.

She's on her fifth now, every two years, all boys so far, miniature replicas of Kennard. The first one's already lost some teeth to hockey, the second held back a grade, the third—the one she was so sure was going to be a girl is—called Robert, and the fourth has just been toilet trained. All this and more she told me over the phone in a rising and falling voice that I don't remember as being hers at all. She made me promise to come and visit her as soon as I got to the Fort.

~

It's late September in Fort McMurray. It's snowed already but it hasn't stayed. The snow and frost have turned all the leaves, lawns are waiting on a raking, hockey nets have been dug out of basement storage and are set off to the side of garages, new face-off circles are painted onto driveways, back-to-school sales are peeling down as Halloween masks and pumpkins sprout in store widows.

It took me a minute to get my bearings. That's never happened to me in the Fort before. This is the first time I've been back in four—closer to five years. It's the longest I've ever been away. The map I've been carrying around in my mind is hopelessly out of date.

I'm on the wrong side of the street—that's all it was. I take a long, narrow look across at Kennard's shop, the false front of his life with Roberta and the kids.

APPLIANCE REPAIR & SERVICE
TRADE-INS WELCOME
WE BUY & SELL

Kennard made the lettering himself, from white electrical tape. I remember the production he made putting it up right after they got married, just about when Roberta was starting to show with their first, just before I left the Fort for Edmonton. I see where some of the tape has peeled away and how the glue behind has left enough of a grimy after-image to still make out the words. It is typical of Kennard to ignore such things.

Kennard is a small businessman, an Elk, who drinks at the Legion, and gives the same little something whenever the Lions or the Kinsmen come calling. Kennard's store is immune to all the seasons of commerce. It is a place for him and his cronies to meet in between hirings and firings to drink coffee laced with the cream of conquest or the bitter taste of deals gone sour.

Kennard's store is divided into two rooms—a showroom and a workshop—by a missing door. Along the west wall, just past the door frame and into the workshop, a wool blanket hides an entrance to a stairwell. In falling oil times like now, times of lay-offs, shutdowns, and foreclosures, Kennard is thankful for the nest above, the four rooms cubed together up the stairwell over the store.

I can tell it's Kennard moving about in the back of the store even through the grimy window. He has a bad left leg; it seems to stop and follow after him like a stray dog making up its mind. I think it's a small miracle—that he's alone and actually at work—until I see a curl of smoke rising from a stool in a corner.

Kennard has tied a cowbell to the jamb of the door; it's his joke of an idea for a bell or chime. He never comes out to see who, if anybody, is there; it's his habit to let his customers find him. His showroom is crammed, packed and piled up like I've never seen before. There are at least two dozen freezers. Two or three are plugged in and working; the rest have rolled-up logs of newspapers wedged into them like fat toothpicks to keep their mouths slightly open. The air in the showroom is pink and silver with specks and flecks of fibreglass.

I recognize the curl of smoke when it slinks into the show-room—another Ferguson, a cousin of Kennard's. About the same age, but this one is already an old-timer.

The North does this to some people: it turns them into old-timers overnight. It has nothing to do with age or long-standing status in the community. An old-timer is a type, a sub-specie, like teenagers into punk, or people who jog in minus-forty.

Old-timers are easily identified by their deep farmer's tans on creased leathery skin: they wear toques or baseball caps and several layers of bargain-bin clothing in all seasons. All old-timers have eyes that back up and cross at a point focused just below your nose or just beyond the horizon.

Kennard's cousin I remember. I remember when he came up to Fort McMurray from Estevan, Saskatchewan. He had his own car and that was enough for some girls to find him cute. Roberta wanted me to double date with him, her and Kennard.

Roberta was so blind crazy over Kennard she couldn't see a blessed thing. Every girl has to draw the line somewhere, and Kennard's cousin—he was it for me.

Kennard's cousin gives me the once, twice over and a slow grin. That's another thing about old-timers, they're not smilers, they grin at you and most have had trouble with their teeth.

"Hey! Hey Kenny," he calls back over his shoulder, "come and take a look-see at who's here."

Kennard wipes his hands against his coveralls and comes, his left leg dragging behind, squinting out into his showroom.

"Hazel? Hazel Jenkings. It's still Jenkings?" He's already peeped at my ring finger. I sense him deciding if he should just shake hands or go for the hug and kiss.

145

I help him decide with a straight arm fully extended.

"You still in Edmonton? Still teaching?" Kennard asks.

He goes clop-clopping into his workshop and yells up the stairwell, "Hey Bobby! Hey Bobby! You've got company."

I've never been a teacher. I work for the School Board in Accounts. I suspect my mother has something to do with why Kennard and most of the people in the Fort think I'm a teacher. I've given up on trying to correct the impression.

"Give her five minutes, Hazel," Kennard says. "She'll give me hell later if you don't give her five minutes now. She'll want to fix herself up a little. She gets to feeling real owly when she's pregnant."

We stand around for a minute with Kennard asking all the stock question and me nodding my answers.

"What are you doing with so many—with all of these freezers?" I ask him.

"The Newfies," Kennard shakes his head, "there's no work."

Kennard's cousin confirms this, "You wouldn't believe how many of the Newfies have up and left. There was one convoy this spring, it alone was two-hundred cars long."

At one time, about one-third of the people in the Fort were from the Maritimes, mostly from Newfoundland. They started to arrive not too long after my father moved us here, and there was a real deluge during the boom, when Syncrude was being built.

"Freezers," Kennard explains, "aren't worth the trouble and the gas it takes to haul them all the way back to Newfoundland. They're practically giving them away. I buy only from my oldest customers; even so, I could've had another fifty or more, easy."

"You should've seen that convoy," Kennard's cousin makes an extravagant sweep with his arm. "They went right by the shop. We counted them—me, Kenny, and little Kenny."

"Lord thunderin' Jesus bye. Where does a Newfie keep all of his money?" Kennard asks, an old joke between cousins. "He buys old cars and keeps them out in his backyard where he can watch them rust."

"Lord thunderin' Jesus bye," Kennard's cousin plays the refrain. "Two hundred cars. All loaded up. Ironing boards strapped to the roofs for your area-dynamics."

Kennard's joking with his cousin but he's not laughing. Neither of them are. Kennard dodges around some of his freezers until he has a clear angle of view out the window of his store.

"Some people went back in the same beaters they came out in. Hard to believe, but true. Lots of 4 x 4s, Jimmys and Broncos, lots of station wagons—those Newfies have big families as a rule. You know how those Newfies like to turn everything into a big to-do. It was sort of like a parade and a funeral all rolled up together in one."

"The original plan was to get an early start and leave the Fort by eight AM," Kennard's cousin grins at me. "But it was well after eleven when they went rolling by here. We could hear them coming for blocks because of the horn-honking, but by the time they got to here they'd quit all that. All of the cars had their headlights on. And they'd dip the lights to salute people they knew on the sidewalk. It was like lightning to go with thunder."

Kennard keeps on staring out the window, until all the cars are out of his mind.

"I'll go up and see how ready Bobby is," he offers.

Kennard's cousin keeps his grin trained on me. His name won't come, and I don't particularly care to dig too deep for it.

Kennard got his leg all mangled by trying to fix something under his cousin's car. The car slipped off its jack or the blocks, something like that. Kennard was always poking around engines. Kids in school used to say he was majoring in Shop. When Roberta and I were in grade nine, Kennard was repeating grade eleven. It was the third grade he had to repeat, and the joke about Kennard was if he ever made it through grade twelve, the principal was going to retire Kennard's locker and his desk.

Kennard was such a greaser, a Neanderthal. His aping would send Roberta and me into giggling fits; in junior high we took pains, we went to great lengths to avoid him.

When Roberta confessed she had a crush on him, I refused to believe her. When she got pregnant halfway through grade twelve, I had no sympathy for her. We had plans. I had plans. I had planned on us leaving the Fort together and on us sharing an apartment in Edmonton.

Roberta's pregnancy gave my mother a because. All of my whys were met with, "Because I don't want you to wind up like your best friend." My mother made it so I couldn't wait to get out of the Fort.

It took some time, but we patched things up. Roberta stays with me in Edmonton whenever she makes one of her massive shopping pilgrimages without Kennard and the kids. Our friendship resumed at a point where we have more or less remained: we trade information. I tell her where the bargains are and she fills me in on the doings and un-doings back in the Fort.

Every time Roberta announced another one on the way, I

would get a plunging feeling of loss mixed up with betrayal. I felt as if her time was pouring through the hourglass; whenever I looked at her big belly and tired eyes, so much more of it was spent. It used to upset me so much, make me angry at Kennard, and at Roberta, to see her so young and so tied down like that.

But now ... when the Kennards of the world ask, "Married yet?" I'm numb as ice.

I have no regrets about leaving the Fort. If I had stayed God knows, by now I might have even started to find the grin on Kennard's cousin attractive.

～

Roberta is nine months pregnant; her due date is "any minute now." She does most of her living in her kitchen. The two of her kids not yet in school are under the table with crayons and scraps of paper. They soon lose interest in me, and Roberta and I settle down to a cup of coffee.

"I shouldn't be drinking this," she smiles, and I see the old— my young Roberta popping out, "but guilt makes a cup of coffee taste so good."

She looks younger than I expected her to look. Her skin is smooth and unlined. She tells me how she's retaining water at a rate, a sure sign for her. She says how she'll be glad to get this one over with. "Nine months is nine months and it doesn't get any shorter with practice."

"Kennard has his heart set on a girl," Roberta sighs. "I'd love one too, but girl or no girl, no matter what we get this time, that's it. I've already made the arrangements," she confides.

"Kennard doesn't know, but I'm having my tubes tied."

We are more comfortable when talking about other people. It doesn't take long to get on to the subject of my mother. When Roberta speaks of my mother, more than half the world away, I see my mother's starring role in an often repeated topic of conversation in the Fort; I hear envy and awe mixed in with pride and surprise.

"Your mom shocked everybody when she just up and left. None of us even knew exactly where between heaven and hell Papua New Guinea was. Little Kenny's grade three class has a project of collecting books and clothes and such to send in care of your mom. She sends them back photos of their pen pals and her hut and the market, things like that."

Roberta says how she'd heard how the house was up for sale. She swallows a big sip of her coffee as if to help her digest the piece of news when I tell her that my mother has gone and signed up for two more years.

"I don't know what-all to do with her stuff," I complain. "She didn't give me a clue about what she wants to keep."

"Get rid of it," Roberta surprises me the way she says it; she's so definite. "I would get rid of it all."

"My mother has tons of stuff," I keep on complaining. "You know what I should have done? I should've just hired somebody. But I can't. I couldn't. She's not—my mother's not ... it's not as if she's dead. I can't stand the thought of some strangers going through it all. Even if she doesn't care—she's still entitled to her privacy."

It's hard to watch Roberta draw herself up out of her chair, slow, slowly as if from a deep well.

"Let me help you with that," I insist, but she's already lumbering off to the sink with the coffee cups. Her two kids come out from under the table and each takes hold of a leg; Roberta sways against and chatters with her towlines. I watch her swollen fingers gently soaping and rinsing the cups; I watch how the water on the draining-board always finds a passage.

Roberta measures her way back from the sink to the table; she lowers herself into her chair with a sharp intake of air. For five to fifteen seconds of eternity, her face is flash-frozen in pain.

"Should I go and get Kennard?"

No, she waves me off. No, with big sweeping xs. Her fingers are so white.

"It's the coffee," she manages a weak smile. "We always have to pay for our sins. Your mom told me that," Roberta says as some colour returns to her face. "When I got pregnant the first time, I went to your mom. Before I told Kennard, before I told you, or anyone."

"I'm not surprised," I lie. "That sounds just like my mom." It doesn't matter, after all this time, but I still feel hurt. Anything, big or small, I would have gone to Roberta with it first.

"Your mom said it wasn't the end of the world. She said it never is. She said I had a choice. She said we always have a choice. I guess she's done gone and proved that. For her to just pick up and go to Papua New Guinea, just like that, after twenty years."

"I just wish," she smiles and I see some more of my Roberta breaking out, "that I could have someone like you, Hazel, to come in and clean up after me."

I think of all the packing up still left to do. "If you don't mind, I have some boxes of books and old toys the kids might like."

"Sure," Roberta nods and settles back into her chair.

Kennard's cowbell clangs, and we can hear his laughing curses mixed up with his cousin's cough and someone else's, a customer or another one of his cronies. They are moving something around, one of those freezers; the dragging rolling sound is amplified up the stairwell like thunder coming closer.

Roberta waits through the noise; hers is a practiced silence. The cowbell clangs some more, somewhere outside an engine starts, and the sound of thunder rolls off.

"I've got to get going," I stand up.

Roberta stirs, a reflex of manners, then settles back into her chair. Her kids and the warm kitchen settle right back down around her.

Whenever someone asks, "Where are you from?" I always give the Fort as home. And as long as my mother was still living here, the Fort was home. If—when you don't have kids, a family of your own, then your parents' home, the home of your childhood remains as your reference point. But if neither of your parents are still living in a place, can you keep on calling it home?

I have no desire to ever live in the Fort again, but what will happen to my childhood, my memories, without the fact of home?

"Hazel," Roberta sees how I've stalled and how I'm fidgeting in her kitchen. "You won't ever be a stranger here, you know."

For a soft moment it is exactly like when we were kids; Roberta knows just what to say and I know just what to do. I go and kneel beside her chair. I take hold of a handful of those fat white fingers. She draws my hand in hers to her, and together we trace circles over the full moon of her belly.

MR. LU'S GARDEN

CAMBODIA WAS BACKSTAGE—the prop room for the Vietnam war; an entrepot over the mountains; a hive for guerrillas to range from on quick stinging missions into Vietnam. It was a place at a time when risk brought reward and dizzying prosperity: In Cambodia, Mr. Lu earned the fortune his father had left China to seek.

Mr. Lu took the giant step up from carpenter to self-employed contractor. During the construction boom years of the sixties, Mr. Lu had the foresight to secure a lucrative corner of the market, primarily in excavation. He bought an imported backhoe to dig out basements, fences, patio decks, and increasingly, swimming pools for the nouveau riche: those black-market geniuses whom he admired and disliked for the way they prospered like fat flies around a skinny water buffalo.

Mr. Lu's home was his showpiece; he and his wife took special pride in it. They believed that the best advertisement for a product was to use it yourself. He made a constant study of American magazines on home improvements and renovations, and he was among the leaders in introducing *customization*. Mr. Lu's basements were all the rage until the exceptionally bad monsoon season of '67. His screened-in back porch became a fixture in all of the better neighbourhoods, but it was his terraced garden with the wishing well that made his reputation.

The garden was his wife's idea, and it was she who suggested a precautionary new way of marketing the basements as bomb shelters thus reviving that end of the business.

The war in neighbouring Vietnam had been going on for so long that Mr. Lu's eldest daughter spoke French and his youngest was taking secretarial English. US Intelligence felt that the most effective solution for an end to the war was to disrupt the lines of supply and called for the bombing of Cambodia. President Nixon agreed.

In November 1969, when the war came to Mr. Lu's home to pay a visit, it did not knock. It showed no respect for Mr. Lu's hard-earned status as a self-employed small contractor. It did not come around cap-in-hand asking at the back door for a job, nor did it come tooting its horn with impatience at the front door for one of Mr. Lu's four attractive teenage daughters. When the war came to Mr. Lu's house, he was trembling in his basement bomb shelter with his wife, his four daughters, two of the young men who were courting his eldest daughter, and the wife and infant son of one of his neighbours.

Mr. Lu's wife had always loved the sound of wind chimes: she kept a pagoda of glass and bamboo suspended in her kitchen window, and she could hear each note, brittle and clear as tears splashing on the Melmac counters of her beautiful (*Better Homes and Gardens* July '65) kitchen. Mr. Lu's four daughters cried in tender unison, reminding him what it was like when they were babies; the two young men could do nothing but fiddle with their hands, and the wife of his neighbour kept her baby pressed to her breasts like a flower between pages of sheet music. Mr. Lu heard only the familiar, what he had long ignored—the metronome of the war, high-pitched, amplified, screaming down.

Of course Mr. Lu had used reinforced steel and good quality brick on the walls of his house; on the roof he had used a new type of rust-resistant galvanize and a brand of creosote sealant that was guaranteed by its manufacturer for life. The war drummed its tune on his roof with all the fury of all the monsoons Mr. Lu had ever heard or imagined.

When the war passed over, Mr. Lu stood shaking, the only leaf in what was left of his wife's terraced garden. His house was a cloud of rubble. The still-smoldering basement that he had so carefully excavated with his backhoe was now completely filled in with the screams of his family. Mr. Lu felt he had never seen such a blue sky before, and he could see how and where a red rash was spreading from east to west in the elongated shape of a water buffalo. When Mr. Lu abandoned the smoking carcass of his house, he took only those facts that he needed for his survival: flies are known carriers of disease, and mosquitoes need blood to feed their young.

～

TORONTO, NOVEMBER 1971

Playing college football is what got Macklin his Draft deferral. But after two years of flunking out and a November birthdate that got picked early in the Lottery, Macklin went north. Armed with a letter from his head coach, clippings from the sports pages of his hometown newspaper, one suitcase and two duffel bags, prayers from his mother, and a tight-lipped stare at some inner horizon from his dad, Macklin left Georgia by bus and by train, journeying for three roundabout days until he reached Canada in the spring.

Macklin felt sure he had it in him to play professional football. He brazened his way into a twenty-one-day tryout with the Toronto Argonauts. Macklin thought he had the team made, too. After the first twenty-one-day trial, they resigned him for another twenty-one quick as ever. A week into the second twenty-one, the Argos brought in four cuts from NFL training camps and billeted them at the same hotel. The way Macklin tells it, the next morning at the hotel breakfast, once he saw those four wolves eat and eat—he knew he was history. The next day, the Argos cut him loose. A handshake, his pay envelope, and the tiniest of candles, "It's a numbers game, up here. The Import Ratio. Keep in shape, you never know ... with injuries."

Later, Macklin would say that he knew right then and there it was the final cut: Peewee, Bantam, Midget, Junior, High School, and College; there was nothing left to bleed.

Macklin found a girl—Sandy, who was willing to sit in the rain under Macklin's personal black cloud and drink his money. She had white, almost alabaster skin, red hair, and quite a thirst. Macklin's shallow well soon went dry.

On the November afternoon of the day of his twenty-first birthday, Macklin awoke. He found himself in a motel room with Sandy, without a cent, and owing a week's room rent to the motel night manager....

～

The motel's faded neon promises a lake view, but Macklin's room is low and crouched at the back. Twin guardrails from an expressway run parallel to infinity along his horizon; in the foreground, his view is framed by concrete columns and venetian blinds. Overnight, freezing rain, then snow, had mixed on the pallet with charcoal exhaust fallout from the expressway; Macklin stares down at the foul droppings of this weather that has congealed on cars, discoloured and cramped like old gravestones in the motel's parking lot.

When Macklin first came up in the spring, Canada hardly even seemed like another country, except for the one exhibition game he played in up in Montréal. So much the same was on TV; The Dairy Queen, Sears, and Famous Recipe Chicken were on every other corner. The snow brought a new resolution to the landscape; it is finally winter, finally a Canada in line with his vague, mostly forgotten geography.

The November sun is weak against the thick-sealed-in motel glass behind which Macklin shivers. He can even make out the tiny pneumatic skid marks of seagulls as they land on the closed lid of the giant garbage bin below his window. His stare is drawn by the surprise of the familiar in an unexpected place: a Georgia *The Peach State* license plate sticking out from the rows of Ontario, *Keep It Beautiful*.

Eighteen had superseded twenty-one as the legal age: You could vote at eighteen, go get drunk at eighteen, go to war for and donate your life to your country at eighteen. Twenty-one, the traditional coming-of-age, had lost most of its luster, but not to Macklin's mother. She wrote a birthday reminder to her Mack, her only boy-child, now that he was a full-grown man, to leave room in his heart for praise and thanks to the Lord. Her letters always gave the family news first, then she'd tell about his friends and any local gossip that came her way. She thought it best he knew, that is, before he came back home and had to hear it all at once—about Henry Green and Eric Johnson.

The town was planning a memorial. Someone had suggested renaming a street, but that was still under hot debate in council. She couldn't help but wonder how different a song would've been sung if they were white boys, and asked the Lord's forgiveness for that, right away. More and more, she was sure her Mack had done the right thing in going up to Canada.

Henry Longfellow Green. And Eric 'The Rambler' Johnson.

Macklin can see them in their too-large uniforms: The Rambler's bucktooth smile and Henry with the worst brush cut in history. He tries to zoom past them, so slicked-down proud in their carefully creased uniforms, to focus in on touch football and pickup basketball, to hear The Rambler's outrageous guaranteed no-fail copping lines, but everything before last spring is blurred. And everything before junior high is now a complete blank.

Macklin shivers again and tries to raise a spit but can't. His morning-after mouth is sandpaper dry, his belly hard and distended. He begins to have trouble breathing. He takes to the throne. Nothing comes to him; nothing leaves him. Macklin squeezes the roll around his midriff; ever since coming up to Canada, he has been steadily gaining weight and alarmingly shedding his past. He figures the weight gain is from not playing ball but still eating as if he were, but he has no answer for what is happening to his past, no ready pounds and inches measure for his loss. In Toronto, he is without familiar comparisons and the underpinning of community; everyone he meets is someone new, and without the attachment of memories, he has no reference points for his emotional geography. He is left with only a vague feeling of grief for the MIA fragments of his high-school friends. His very sense of loss is suspect, an undiagnosed allergy triggered by uncertain cause. His tolerance grows as events in letters from home lose meaning. His past is a receding radio signal, distorting in and out of the tangle and immediacy of his hand-to-mouth existence.

Stuck on the throne, Macklin runs water to encourage things, but to no avail. His melon belly is so hard it hurts to hold. He can hear it gurgle over running water like a steam boiler. At last he feels a wave rise in the backwater near his kidneys. Something dislodges, then heaves, through his small, then his large, intestine; it goes on its hurting way up the back of his lungs. The dry, sour taste of guilt chases shame up his windpipe to lodge behind his teeth and gums.

He cannot breathe in. Macklin grips his belly and bears down on the toilet seat. The lump settles back down.

Stasis. He still cannot breathe. No air in.

Skin is the largest organ of the body. Macklin feels his burn. No air.

Macklin tries and tries. He can make his mouth open. He can scream. But he cannot inhale. The lack of incoming air reduces his scream to a high, inaudible pitch in seconds. Over on the bed, Sandy stirs but does not wake. Macklin reels over to the window; his blows are soft rain against the hard glass, attracting only the cockeyed attention of the seagulls.

In desperation now, Macklin stumbles back to the wash-room. If he can only empty his stomach and rid himself of that lump, he knows that would make room. For air!

He has an idea; he will force himself to vomit. He will stick his hand down his throat, up to the elbow if necessary, and make himself puke. Dry heaves. That's as far as he can reach. He tries and tries, squeezing his belly up with one hand and grop-ing down his throat with the other.

No air!

Macklin looks in the bathroom mirror. His face has set into an open-mouth scream, his skin already blue. Macklin knows that he only has seconds left. Sandy is his last hope. He lunges over to the bed. Macklin gives Sandy a desperate shake; she rolls away deeper under the covers. Macklin has no more strength. He starts to black out. He collapses onto the bed on top of Sandy.

"Hey! Shit! Man!" Sandy yells.

It is the last thing that Macklin dimly heard.

~

Jerry Elias, the motel night manager, was hurried out of his sleep by a woman's screams.

The screams cut off abruptly, like an engine gone suddenly dead. Jerry stumbles into his pants and hurries down to Macklin's room, fearing the worst. The screams resume in a new, higher pitch, each curse clear and distinct as glass breaking.

A naked girl, chalk-white with rage, flings the door open. An overpowering smell pours out from the dank, airless room. Jerry recognizes it right away: eagle shit.

Jerry closes the door and bug-eyes past the naked girl into the room over to the bed where Macklin is beached, his gulping snores rising and falling, lapping like the sound of waves about the tiny room. At first, Jerry thinks that Macklin's face is fixed into the widest grin, then he sees the way Macklin's flesh is drawn taut all over. Gingerly, he probes and pokes a shoulder, an earlobe, tickles then slaps the balls of Macklin's feet.

Macklin is tangled and stuck, at every turn, a giant tar baby. Jerry clinically studies the mess. He divides the dark stains into categories, looking for eagle droppings among the excrement, the urine, and the dark clots of blood.

Sandy stops her ranting long enough to give Jerry a look of pure disgust. She shoves him aside and launches herself at Macklin, smacking into him as hard as she can. She lands on both of her knees in the small of his back. A single grunt interrupts Macklin's snores. Jerry grabs her by the wrists and straight-arms her away from the bed. Her curses turn to fearful tears.

Jerry is drawn by a glint from the darkest, angriest clot of blood. From it, he separates with a wad of toilet paper a blue-white stone. The stone is oval, solid, and hard. About the size of a pigeon's egg. The blue and the white are in stratified swirls. The markings could mean anything; Jerry sees tightly folded wings.

~

Jerry Elias is from Allentown, Pennsylvania, where his step-father operates an independent drugstore and has shares in a bowling alley. His mother still works in the beauty salon next to the drugstore. His stepfather has a sister married to a man in Toronto.

In 1970, Jerry was attending pharmacy school in New Jersey to please his mother and out of respect for his stepdad. He was doing fine in pharmacy school. Back in Allentown there was a girl he liked, whom he felt liked him back.

Uncle Sam called. It's urgent, he pointed. Come, he crooked a finger at Jerry: We Need You, Now.

Jerry could have pressed his college deferment. His stepfather knew a doctor who was ready to swear to a bad back or trick knee, if that was what Jerry was sure, really sure, he wanted.

Jerry was no longer sure about any of it. He had begun to dream about eagles, constantly. Not the majestic National Geographic soaring creatures, but stylized Egyptian hieroglyphic eagles, German army medallion eagles, E Pluribus Unum eagles. For weeks on end he dreamt only of parts of eagles: bald spots, glaring-eye stares, ruffled wing-feathers. Soon he began to see the shape of an Eagle in cloud formations, under streetlights, in the cool shadows cast by store awnings on his afternoon way into his summer job at the drugstore.

Each day in August, a darkening feather, a toenail hardening to a talon, Jerry's Eagle gained substance until one Thursday evening, as he was making a vanilla milkshake for Brenda Kennedy who worked in the beauty salon next door, while she was on her break, with an extra scoop, just the way she liked it, his Eagle landed in front of the drugstore. It hopped off a stretch between two parking metres, and then it tucked in its wings and fixed a wooden Indian stare right through the drugstore window at Jerry.

Jerry poured Brenda Kennedy's vanilla milkshake onto the arborite counter in front of her, down her white uniform, and spilling down her now-vacant, spinning red stool. Jerry was supposed by all to have had a long-standing crush on Brenda. He never even heard her astonished yelps or saw her sad, surprised tears.

Uncle Sam grew testy. He felt sure that Jerry was getting into the business of pulling his own teeth and began to insist. Jerry's stepfather felt that Jerry should make a fresh start. Right away. His mother agreed, with love and a puzzled heart. His stepfather called his sister up in Toronto. Her husband knew some people in the motel business.

Jerry's condition followed him to Toronto, cloaking him in delicious rumour; he was said to have connections to the Mafia. One smug maid had it from the highest source that he was on the run, on ice; something criminal or at least tragic had happened, and he was to be kept out of the public's eye at all costs.

Freed from eagle-infested sleep, Jerry spent his nights balancing the daily take and drawing pictures of eagles. After a year in the clear Toronto air, Jerry was down to doodling feathers and beaks in the margins of his accounts receivable. He was promoted with a ten dollar a week raise, and given a dark, unrentable room for a live-in office and the title of night manager.

Jerry expropriated the row of dark, unused rooms at the back of the motel and let them out off the books, most often to other Americans in displaced transit from the war. Once, Abbie Hoffman had slept in the very room that Macklin was having his breakdown in. Jerry also lent money, at ten percent per week, twenty percent for anything over one hundred dollars to a maximum of five hundred dollars. Macklin was a repeat customer.

Later, while cleaning up after Macklin, Jerry found another stone in the sheets—about as big, and with the same blue-white striations. He placed the two stones on a bed of Styrofoam chips and sealed them up tight in a Mason jar.

～

NOVEMBER 1975
PULAU MIMPI (ISLAND OF DREAMS), MALAYSIA

A room full of flies. And thin mosquitoes.

Someone has divided this room with chalk marks on the floor; people are queued within the trail of these broken dashes that lead to a row of desks. The flies are based in overcrowded colonies on the ceiling, thick enough to give the humming impression that the twin suspended fans are about to whir into operation. The mosquitoes are in two queues of suspended belief.

The Canadians are here. The French over there. Four Australians sweat in concentric circles. The Americans have their own building (and, it is rumoured, with air conditioning that works). At the back of the queues, two parallel lines of chairs complete the "I" formation of the room. Just inside and just beyond the door, six UN soldiers are planted like pot-bellied palms. Outside, the queue resumes in a hesitant shuffling fashion, dwindling into the sprawl of the refugee compound. Behind the sparkling newness of barbed wire is the neat disorder of a lab experiment gone awry: barracks with corrugated patches of colour where mutant rats have chewed through the insulation. Cook-pots converted from kerosene drums are slow to boil in front of the bent-over worried and watchful eyes of women; clusters of near-naked men flex and gingerly take inventory of their diminished bodies in the light of the morning sun; children pluck and strum the barbed-wire fence, begging at each and every footstep of those who pass outside the compound.

The Canadian official is late this morning. To get to work he must park and walk past the children, along the long west side of the perimeter. He knows that he could choose to do like some of the others, like the Ozzies, and carpool. But his staff car is a fiercely guarded privilege.

"Keep the car." His predecessor had been adamant. "Whatever you do. Don't go and get talked into a driver. We're here for Immigration, not Employment. You must keep control of the car!"

He was surprised; Pulau Mimpi is such a tiny island. "Did you," he asked the man he was replacing, "do much driving?"

"No, no." The outgoing official shook his head vigorously. "You'll want to know that you can go—that you can always go for a drive. You see. You'll see...."

Today, as every day, when he passes the compound, a bubble forms, a question (Where is the end of the line?), the bilious taste of which will stay with him all day. He has tried but he has never mastered the Gallic shrug of official, professional dismissal. But today, at last, he understands about the car.

And he resolves that starting today, yes, he will take a drive. Once a day. He will let One through. Each day. He will grant safe passage through the paper minefield to One.

One: Mr. Lu is more than forty, less than fifty, a slight man lessened even more by the war. His hair has thinned from black to grey and silver. Malnutrition has clouded the whites of his eyes and touched his skin, along with nicotine, a curious shade of amber. There is a slackness to the flesh around his neck, as if in apposition to the tightness around his eyes.

Mr. Lu is bagasse, one of the unwanted by-products of the war, abandoned to the squalid limbo of Pulau Mimpi. He is unable to fit into any of the spaces—no sponsor, no family, no skills, not even a disability—on any of the official forms.

Every day Mr. Lu joins in the queue out of habit. There is nothing heroic or romantic about Mr. Lu's wish to survive: It was not a romantic war at all, less about the will to live, more about the wont to die.

Mr. Lu sustains by counting. He is a counter: the slapping sound of waves against the cork of a boat, the number of places ahead of him in the line, each chain-link, every spark of barbed-wire is double-counted until it is impossible for him to think.

In this way, with his head full of numbers, he is able to blot, to drown out the metronome of the war: his wife's wind chimes, his daughters' voices, the two helpless young men, and a young mother clutching her crying baby to her like an accordion.

Today Mr. Lu's count is One ... tick, one skipped heartbeat, one Canadian official's quixotic act, one checkmark of compassionate sanity-saving defiance sets Mr. Lu's wind-mill in motion.

~

TORONTO, LATE NOVEMBER 1975

Sandy Bradley was just thirteen when her parents died. Sandy ended up living with an aunt who was childless. It happens this way sometimes—the very presence of one child stirs something and brings on another. Her aunt, barren for so long, soon gave birth to and began to dote on a daughter of her own.

At fourteen, Sandy ran away for the first time. Her aunt discreetly took her to see a psychiatrist. The doctor told Sandy's aunt what she already knew. He said, "Sandy is a hormonal grenade ready to explode."

Around school Sandy became known as a sufferer of fits and spells. Some parents took to threatening their children with "a fate worse than that Sandy."

She ran away, often—but was always caught and reeled back. Sandy vowed that the minute she turned legal, she would cut herself adrift. On the morning of her eighteenth birthday, she hitchhiked her way to Toronto. Macklin was as far away as she could get.

～

"When a man starts off by shitting on you," Sandy trots out an old punchline for Jerry, "there's nowhere to go but up from there."

She's at Jerry's place. In a sticky mood, bitching, recalling old times. After four years, she is the one who's the most surprised that she and Macklin are still together. Not that it has gotten any easier, certainly not now with her belly big and late in an uncomfortable pregnancy. Her alabaster skin has turned to white porcelain; it's as if the rest of her colour has drained down into her belly.

Sandy pokes at her swollen feet and watches as the dimples slowly refill. Jerry makes sympathetic noises and offers to open a window.

Jerry is now an almost-Certified Accountant; he put his nights at the motel to use by sending away for courses from the back of a book of matches. Sandy hears the origins of the set speech he will tell his children and grandchildren: how he worked two jobs and studied all night long to pay his own brave way in a new country.

"What's keeping our birthday boy?" Jerry asks, in the lull that comes to people when they've lost touch and their conversation returns inevitably back to their common denominator.

"He's over in Hamilton," Sandy says. "He's with Dick Gregory."

"The comedian?" Jerry asks.

"Yes," Sandy smiles and parrots a speech, "Macklin says not to call him that. Mack says Mr. Gregory don't like being called a comedian. A comedian-turned-activist. Mr. Gregory told Mack it's just the way the media tries to tear him down and discredit whatever he has to say."

Jerry grins at her and shrugs. After he left the motel business he no longer had or kept up any connections to that scene—the loose and fast alliances built on the displacement of war, held together by newsletters that folded after one or two issues detailing the latest atrocities; by wives and girlfriends, the go-betweens to Back Home; or patrons of coffee shops and certain in restaurants identified by the uniform of bulletin-board T-shirts and the ironic overstatement of army surplus khaki; by talk and more talk, of CIA involvement, of Amnesty, of going Back Home versus the angst of Staying Put.

Jerry had joined those who moved out of Cabbagetown and the Annex, away from crash pads and communal living, out to Don Mills and Mississauga, into bungalows and split-level sunken living-room success.

Macklin had found a place in the scene. His strong right arm got him work as a bouncer at nightclubs; he delivered newsletters and stuck up posters for concerts; when businesses expanded out of basements and garages into boutiques and malls, Macklin was there to load boxes, paint walls, and lay carpet. He became a fixture in the pedestrian mall on Yonge Street, where he kept an eye and a steering hand out for new arrivals from the States.

When it was discovered that Macklin had an enormous appetite for guilt, he became a dinner guest of choice in the sandblasted homes of several small "l" liberals. He slept with wives on request and played racquetball with husbands. He took to the role of stand-in at good causes. He became an acceptable excuse: "So Sorry, We Can't Make It, But Here's Macklin."

This led to a series of tangential intersections with the famous. It was Macklin who went to the all-night drugstore for the Midol when that folksinger had such bad cramps; Macklin who went downtown for the Sunday New York Times for that poet everyone thought would become important; Macklin who checked and toted luggage; Macklin who drove them to and waited until speaking engagements were over. Macklin who was missing out on his own birthday get-together while he took Dick Gregory to Hamilton.

~

"How many white women do you know? Answer their door to a stranger wearing only a negligee and carrying just their driver's license?"

Dick Gregory has his audience on the edge of their seats and he is determined to keep them there. "That's exactly what the media says that Patty Hearst did."

Dick is a slim lion prowling the floor of the shallow amphi-theater. More than half the McMaster University audience is black, undergrads from the West Indies. They've come out curious to hear Dick Gregory, the black American comedian, the celebrity.

The Vietnam War is over. It's a non-issue. This crowd has no questions about the Cause or the Movement. They want to know how Dick Gregory made it Big. About his fasting, the tactic that gained him notoriety.

"What do you give to a man who has everything?" Dick knows the sort of crowd he's working. "What do you give to the most powerful man in the world? Watergate. His own soap opera."

Dick's quips keep the crowd off-balance; he follows his black humour leads with short, jabbing localized quasi-facts. "At least one-million dollars a day leaves this city and goes to war, every day. The Pentagon thinks that Hamilton, Ontario is a parts depot."

Macklin, perched on the highest tier at the back, enjoys the way Mr. Gregory works the crowd.

"It's a known fact," Dick nods vigorously, "that a good war heats up the economy. A good economy means jobs. Jobs for all of you when you graduate. Unless it's a nuclear war. Then you can quit worrying. Never mind about those term papers. You can forget those exams. Talk about your final exam."

When Dick throws it open to questions, Macklin thinks about going on ahead to warm up the car. Sandy's sure to be upset. He's late enough already and he still has to take Mr. Gregory back to his hotel.

"Fasting," Dick Gregory says in answer to a question from a short, chubby girl, "has some interesting side effects. Vibes. I start to pick up on vibes after a while. You a Virgo?"

The chubby girl nods yes, astonished.

"And you," Dick points, "you're a Pisces. Right?"

He's right again. A buzz goes through what's left of the crowd. Macklin chuckles; he's heard about this. That Mr. Gregory has some kind of second sight.

Dick underplays the scene; he tells what's left of the crowd, a handful-and-a-half of the curious, more about vibes, about the clarity of mind, the Zen-like plateau that he reaches when fasting. Macklin signals that he's going to ready the car. Dick holds up two fingers in a v, then pulls one down. Macklin waits.

"About twenty-eight, twenty-nine days into a fast," Dick says in answer to another question, "I get a last shit."

Dick has a way of looking; he has a look, something luminous about the whites of his eyes. He looks directly at Macklin.

"The tail end of everything that's left in your system comes out in one last shit. That shit is the stinkiest, the ugliest, the hardest, the hurtingest shit. But once you get that shit out, man, the rest is easy."

Macklin smiles, a tight-lipped smile. As tight as the lid on a certain Mason jar.

~

Sandy and Jerry talk until late about old times: the echo of concerts attended, chance meetings with so and so on the subway, until their words are wishes blown out from the candles on Macklin's birthday cake.

"Did I tell you—I'm Landed now?" Jerry the almost-Certified Accountant has already revised the sum of his past. "I'm getting my citizenship soon," he says. "It makes sense for business. I can't picture myself back in Allentown."

"Congratulations." Sandy calls him a "Canuck."

"Where's Mack?" Sandy begins to cry. What she really wants is to do Things For Herself. And she wishes that everyone would quit calling her Sandy. How she hates that name, and to please call her Cassandra.

Jerry strokes her cheek and says it's a very pretty name; he tries it out a few soft times.

Sandy invites Jerry to feel the baby kick, to help protect the circle of her big belly.

Sandy will have a hard labour. She will have to be induced. On Boxing Day. A boy. She will name him Wesley Jerome, with pride and no protest from Macklin.

SPRING 1978

During the reign of the smiling peanut farmer from Georgia word crossed the border. The general amnesty was for real.

Some of the very first to arrive in Canada, those who had

173

pined the longest while feeding on the strength of their convictions, became giddy with nostalgia and were among the first to leave. Those with shallow new roots left without trauma. The ones in the middle ground, like Macklin, had the hardest time deciding to uproot. It took all of the pull of his mother's letters, more years of twisting and untangling from Sandy, for Macklin to leave.

There was a brief time in the backwash of the bicentennial, under the wave of the flag, when the patriotic spirit was stretched far enough to accommodate even those who had detoured around their version of injustice to Canada. This warm updraft of relief fueled by popular sentiment was short-lived.

Macklin missed it. He returned to an America eager to forget and more that willing to revise. *Coming Home* won the Oscar for best picture in 1978. Mythmakers were working overtime on epic-sized Technicolour postmortems of the living-room war. The scene had shifted to other causes—something old, something new in nightly TV terrors: Israel and Palestine rushed to fill the vacuum left by the pullout from Vietnam. Iran began to dominate the footage on the shrunken head with innovative and sustained acts of terror.

After Vietnam: America surfaced too quickly and got the bends.

~

Macklin left Montgomery early in the morning on the last leg of his journey. He crossed the state line into Georgia and by mid-afternoon he was almost home. He busied himself on the long drive down by taking inventory of his past. By all counts he knew that some pieces were still missing and he could no longer separate the true facts of his youth from the supposes he and Sandy had devised to fill in the blanks.

Familiar territory, at last. Turtle Hill. At the turnoff at Three Roads Corner, down into the plane of the low valley, Macklin can see where his folks' place is nestled against the rise down at the other end. As he approaches the house it seems smaller and not only because the trees are so much bigger.

At the side of the house, two lines of washing are paused like square dancers at a dress rehearsal, waiting for a fresh quiver to be set in swaying motion. Someone is out back in the yard.

Macklin's mother is scattering corn mash from a big bowl. She waits until her chickens flit towards her, then she flings the mash in a wide arc. She hears a car enter her driveway and she comes around from behind the kitchen to see who. When she sees that it is her Mack, she freezes. Then she flings the rest of the corn high into the air. It comes to earth like a rain of gold.

～

Pearline was two times a widow before she even turned thirty. Now she couldn't give it away. No man in Turtle Hill or in any of the surrounding counties would even think about touching Pearline.

"My my," Pearline fans herself. "My, he's so big and so strong and he's so buck handsome," is what Pearline thinks as she eyes Macklin up and down in church, his first Sunday back, him standing there so tall and proud next to his mother. Pearline blushes at the thoughts she thinks right there in church! But she knows she isn't the only one there with eyes, and under her widow's veil her face is set and determined.

It took Pearline until Easter.

Macklin's mother and Pearline volleyed long and hard. How could her Mack come all this way after all these long years and place such a thorn in his mother's side?

Pearline did her lobbing from the baselines; she made sure to always have cold Bud in her fridge and get the barbecue going before the Sunday NFL games.

Macklin slowly settled back into the Georgia earth. He went to church only on occasions and into town only when it was absolutely necessary. He put his strong arms to work on his father's farm and divided his nights between his mother's house and the widow Pearline's bed.

Men his age or a little older steered a wide path around him. In older folk's gossip he was "the boy who went up to Canada during that business over in Vietnam." Among teenagers, Macklin enjoyed the curious sort of cool respect reserved for antiheroes. One of those teenage boys was a younger brother and spitting image of Eric 'The Rambler' Johnson. Every time Macklin saw him, something inside him would give a jump and hurt for an instant.

Two years to the day after Macklin got back, his father had a stroke. It shattered most but not all of the filament in him. Broken glass was in his stare and splinters in his wife's heart.

At first, Macklin's mother offered up bartering prayers to the Lord to make her husband whole again; then, as time dragged by, her hopes turned to sorrowful pleas to grant him eternal rest. Her prayers were answered the next February.

Pearline, much experienced in the art of widowing, proved herself to be true and staunch to Macklin's mother. The bond between the two women was all the more strong for their earlier prickly distance. They launched a double-barreled effort from a united front. Before the year was out, Macklin and Pearline went up and saw a Justice of the Peace in Atlantic City. The men in the district gave Macklin an even wider berth.

His mother's loud sighing prayers were now reserved for her one last wish before her reward, grandchildren. She collected her all-too-few artifacts of "little Wesley so far away in Canada" and gave them prominent display in her living room.

Macklin never talked about Wesley or the years he spent up in Canada. His mother could only guess at what was in those fat legal-looking envelopes, sent by registered mail, that Macklin would have to make a trip into town to sign for.

Macklin's mother concentrated her efforts on Pearline. Pearline already had two children of her own, thank you, neither one of whom ever saw their daddy alive. She flat-out refused to tempt fate again.

Pearline never made it her business to find out about Macklin's time in Canada. If her Mack never brought it up, then she wasn't going to be the one to ask. Quite frankly, it made her uneasy. When she and her mother-in-law got to talking about Macklin's time away, it was always in a hush and only for reference—a family secret, a closed case, as if Macklin had been to prison and paid his debt.

One blue and white November morning, Macklin's mother was out in her backyard with Pearline helping her put her wash out to dry. Sheets and dresses were limp and sullen waiting for a breeze. Down the rise a cloud of dust signals a car coming, and Pearline thinks rightly that it might be the mail. A sudden squall of wind sets the wash to jumping and twisting on the line, a cold wind that sends Macklin's mother and her chickens scurrying for cover.

Pearline volunteers to go around front and check on the mail. She weighs the envelope with the tiny stamp of the English queen's head in the upper-right-hand corner. Pearline can see Macklin in the kitchen. His mother is fixing to pour hot coffee. The cold wind cuts straight through Pearline's sweater and the print of her cotton dress, chilling the sweat under her armpits and between her heavy breasts. Macklin comes and stands with his cup of coffee in the kitchen doorway.

As Pearline begins to walk towards Macklin, he disappears. All she sees is the steam rising from his coffee cup. She stops. It's just a trick of the light. But Pearline feels goose-bumps rise all over her skin and she knows that her shivers have nothing and everything to do with that cold Canada wind.

～

At first Mr. Lu was lonely, but then his quiet life took on new meaning. In those first new years in Canada, everyone in his community of refugees were still deafened by the hum of the metronome: they could neither stop talking nor thinking of the war. At social events, each new arrival recounted old horrors, and the nightmare ethics of survival played on in a loop of old terrors, hidden messages, and missed choices.

Mr. Lu stepped forward to play the important role of wise

uncle. He reminded them that the mosquito needs blood to feed its young. And when the community began to coalesce around ceremony and old rituals, he became a living totem, a reminder of forgotten values—his presence in demand at ceremonies, counted on at births and weddings for protocol; at funerals, it was left to him to say the right things.

At the head table of a wedding banquet, Mr. Lu was paired with a newly arrived widow—a vivacious woman, thin and wound up like the hand-rolled cigarettes she smoked constantly. Hepatitis had a lot to do with why she looked so much older than her forty-six years. In her laughter, Mr. Lu heard enough to guide him into the orbit of her arms in perpetual motion, sending clouds of smoke rising like butterflies to surround and invade, to awake and capture his heart.

After a few shorts months, they were toasting and feasting at a wedding banquet of their own. Mr. Lu felt a double happiness with his new wife. Together, he knew with all certainty, they could look forward and that he could finally face looking back.

~

Out West used to mean Vancouver. Kitsilano, in the inner city, was the headquarters of a flourishing scene with a rash of boutiques spreading out along Broadway and Fourth until the purists left for Saltspring Island, as communal crash pads were renovated into suites, and equity changed from a philosophical to a mortgage statement. Out West took on the generic, the Canadian meaning: anyplace west of Winnipeg.

The Big Oil Boom drew Jerry out west, to Edmonton. He

started his own accounting firm, then branched out into any and every pie his fingers could reach.

Sandy was already out west, in Banff, working as a cook and sometimes waitress. She lived in communes, with a mixed collection of strict vegetarians, college dropouts, first-time beard growers, women who never shaved their legs or armpits, and all those who backpacked through Europe on five dollars a day.

Jerry and Sandy got together by chance (only now it was called synchronicity) at the Banff Folk Festival.

Jerry was in Banff to buy a stake in a motel.

Sandy was paler than Jerry remembered. Her red hair stood out all the more.

Sandy had so much to talk about. Jerry always knew how to listen. She saw a lot of things in Jerry that she didn't remember. And a lot of what she saw she liked. A night of reminiscing ended up in Jerry's bed. They both claimed surprise at the way Things Turn Out.

Wesley was hardly shy with Jerry at all. And Jerry showed a whole new side with Wes. Sometimes Sandy would watch the two of them playing and feel so scared. All the lessons of her life had taught her that she was not entitled to such happiness.

Jerry's accounting business prospered in the downturn after the oil boom. He had a flair for bankruptcies. With Sandy's encouragement, Jerry opened a correspondence with Macklin about the possibility of legally adopting Wesley. Jerry felt his life soar, but then he started finding feathers, eagle droppings.

Cracks began to appear in Sandy's porcelain skin. Sandy clutched at all miracles: yeast, roughage, low sodium, apricot pits. She spent the best part of a year commuting to Fernie, BC, studying macrobiotics. Her red hair will be shaved down to peach fuzz, bald spots dabbed with gel for the pad-paws of electrodes until blue alabaster returns to her porcelain skin, betraying each erosion—every crack a cat's cradle that widens then entangles to form the box canyon that closes on her from within.

~

NOVEMBER

Jerry picked Macklin up at the airport in a white Thunderbird. Macklin had to look twice to recognize him. A lot of the weight Jerry has gained shows on his face. His lips and the corners of his mouth are hidden under the heavy droop of a moustache.

Jerry's red eyes are full of questions. On the way in from the airport, he animatedly tries to engage Macklin, to prepare him for what's ahead.

"When Sandy went in for treatment," Jerry says, "Social Services got involved. As far as they're concerned, I'm not Wesley's natural father. I can't even prove Sandy and me are common law. Now Wesley must sleep at a foster home. It would finish Sandy if she knew."

Macklin stares flatly out the window. Snow is falling and Macklin thinks how cold it is up here. It was so hot in Dallas where he had to change planes. He thinks how it's so easy to get so far away so fast these days.

"You know," Jerry continues, "if it wasn't for the one social worker, they wouldn't even let the boy out to go and see his mother at the Cross."

"The Cross?" Macklin asks.

"The Cross Cancer Institute," Jerry replies.

Macklin breathes and expels his nod.

"Have you given much thought to the adoption papers?" Jerry immediately wishes he could somehow rephrase that blurted question.

"I wish we could have cleared this up with Sandy before." Jerry has to try and find out where Macklin stands. "All I want is what's best for Wesley. Have you decided yet?"

Macklin has turned to stare out his window where suburbs now appear as if in a mirage, veiled by the steadily falling snow along the penumbra of the horizon. Jerry's white Thunderbird fishes in and out of closing traffic; up ahead fingers of the city's downtown poke into view wrapped in a blurred halo of white gauze.

⌒

"Traumatized lungs," a doctor explains to Mr. Lu. "Years of malnutrition and heavy smoking." The doctor has other suspicions. "A biopsy has revealed evidence of a massive and repeated exposure to carcinogenic chemicals."

That is why he is asking for Mr. Lu's permission, "when the time comes ... for the chance to help others, for an autopsy."

Mr. Lu's English is not so good. He does not understand all of the doctor's words. But he understands death and dying. And he is an expert at waiting. Each morning, every morning, for weeks into months into an eternity, he comes to count the tiles on the floor, the dimples in the paint on the walls, the crossing lines on the ceiling—to wait for his new wife to die.

This morning the tone of the doctor's words tell him one thing: his wait is almost over.

⁓

Macklin is in another corner of the waiting room being given a lesson in the grammar of the language used on the terminally ill: "diminished capacity," "marginal attrition," "sustained regression."

The doctor tries to prepare Macklin; "Chemotherapy is like fighting fire with pinpoints of fire."

After weeks of rehearsal Jerry knows this script by rote. He and Mr. Lu are onto the routine of the place. They know that the nurses are readying Mr. Lu's wife and that they will come and call Mr. Lu next. Then it's Sandy's turn. For her tracheal shunt to be drained. For her to be rotated so her bed sores don't deepen, for her to be propped up and readied for her visitors.

Mr. Lu is intently cutting the covers off some old Reader's Digests. Wesley hovers around Mr. Lu, pleased to be a magician's assistant.

"Ah-ar, ah-ar, ah-ar," Mr. Lu demonstrates how with his scissors.

Wesley takes the finished cutting and carefully folds it into a Chinese lantern which he adds to his pile of treasure stowed under an end table in a corner.

Wesley exaggerates every motion in his game with Mr. Lu. And he makes every attempt to avoid Macklin. But he can't. He can't help or stop his eyes from landing on him.

Macklin meets, but can't get Wesley to hold, his gaze. There's no mistaking, even though Wesley's peppercorn hair is tinged with red and the map of his skin shows different shades of brown, the boy looks just like him. He's tall for his age, big hands, he's got the makings of an End or a Lineman, Macklin thinks. Wesley grows even more self conscious under inspection and concentrates on his game with Mr. Lu.

Mr. Lu has told Wesley that he attends school, for his English. Wesley assumes that Mr. Lu's school is like his own and wants to know what Mr. Lu did over his summer holidays.

"In the summertime I like to go fishing." Mr. Lu replies. "But my wife, she say, I must have a garden. A garden is many, many work. Too many hard work. I tell her this. Too many, too many. But she say, 'No Way, Lu! You get busy and plant!'

"So I grow the carrots, the lettuce, the tomato, the beets. All good. A garden is very good. You like the potato? The potato is easy, very easy to grow."

"How big was your garden?" Wesley asks.

"Twenty meters so and twenty-five meters so," Mr. Lu uses the waiting room for a measure, he points and paces off rows of peas and corn. Wesley skips along besides him.

Wesley and Mr. Lu finish seeding and dividing the room. Mr. Lu cuts out blank signs on which Wesley draws the appropriate vegetable.

"Mr. Lu?" Wesley wants to know, "How much food did you grow in your garden?"

"Many many," Mr. Lu answers.

"Did you eat it all up?"

"No," Mr. Lu says softly. Slowly he shakes his head, "No."

"How come?" Wesley insists.

Mr. Lu brushes his grey and silver hair to the side with his hand.

"How come?" Wesley asks again.

"Wesley!" Jerry calls sharply.

Mr. Lu holds his hand palm up and waves Jerry off.

"My wife, she no eat. She say she only want to see my garden grow. To see my garden grow is plenty food enough for her, she say."

"Will you have a garden next summer?" Wesley asks eagerly.

Mr. Lu runs his hand over Wesley's head and forces himself to smile, "Maybe."

"If you have a garden, Mr. Lu? Can I come and work?"

Mr. Lu has no answer.

Wesley returns to drawing his pictures of vegetables. Mr. Lu quietly cuts more squares. Jerry fights to keep his red eyes open. Macklin closes his while trying to sort through his memories. They all inhale the deep silence that overrides even the antiseptic smell of the waiting room.

A nurse comes and calls Mr. Lu. He rises, tucks his shirt into his pants, and gives a quaint half-nod half-bow to Macklin and Jerry. He claps Wesley on the back, "Aye-bye, I see you soon."

"Sandy will be ready next," Jerry states. "You want to go in first?"

Macklin exhales another of his long, slow nods. Wesley remains on the floor, playing with his cutout vegetables, stealing glances every so often at Macklin. Jerry and Macklin take turns sitting, pacing, or standing by the window.

"You ever think about it, Mack?" Jerry asks.

"Vietnam?" Macklin guesses right.

"PBS was running a retrospective." Jerry says. "'American Involvement.' 'A police action.' Do you remember that? God!

"There's war on PBS all the time. The irritating thing about Vietnam on TV," Jerry continues, "is they always make it seem so goddamn glorious. It's hard enough to compare atrocities without having to separate what's real from what's not."

Macklin's attention is focused on Wesley. What he is trying to remember are the baby years in Toronto.

"It never ends," Jerry rubs his red eyes, "Vietnam."

"It's like a virus. When you think you've got it beat, it mutates and comes at you with sharper teeth. Like Legionaries' disease. Nobody knows the cause or the cure and no one gets too concerned. Once in a while you hear about a little outbreak. Someone comes up from the States to do a magazine piece, or somebody from the Movement surfaces with a book and does the rounds of the TV talk shows.

"A couple of years ago my company lost a bid on a contract. I found out the reason why later. I'm considered a security risk. In a file somewhere, I'm a draft dodger."

Wesley has inched his collection of cutout vegetables towards Macklin and Jerry.

Macklin keeps trying, but he can't get Wesley to look at him.

Jerry's red eyes burn into the floor. "How about you Mack? Did you manage an escape from it? Back there in Georgia on your sleepy farm?"

Macklin keeps on staring at Wesley playing with his paper cutouts on the floor. After a long while, he clears his throat and tries to put a shape to his reply.

"I still can't remember … things. Jerry. Everything is faded for me. I'm never sure what's been made up or not."

Macklin has no more to say but there's so much more that he would like to know. What was Wesley like as a baby? Was he always big for his age? How is he? In school? With other kids? At sports?

Macklin looks into Jerry's red eyes, into two pinpoints of another question.

"Jerry," Macklin says in a low growl, "I don't know. About the boy."

Wesley doesn't quite hear Macklin's words, but he knows he's in the question and looks up. This time it's Macklin who averts his eyes.

"Christ! Will you look at the pair of us?" Jerry mutters and slumps back into his chair.

A white sail hovers near the doorway; Macklin gets up and follows the nurse to Sandy's room.

～

"Sandy, Sandy," the nurse sings out. "You have a new visitor."

Macklin edges over to the side of the bed and stops.

"Just talk to her like normal." The nurse sees his confusion and offers, "You could try rubbing her cheeks, sometimes they seem to respond to that."

"Sandy, Sandy," Macklin follows the nurse's example. He traces the silver-blue in her face. Her skin feels cool and smooth like condensation on a glass. Her eyes are fixed open, wide and unfocused. Sandy's skin is bleached the papery colour of a weeping birch in winter.

The nurse meets his look of confusion. She gives Macklin an explanation of coma; she defines the differences between "shallow" and "catatonic." Sandy's vital signs have waned, but it's impossible to say, weeks, months, minutes....

Macklin looks down at Sandy. He begins to have some trouble breathing. He feels his throat constrict. He inhales, one swallow and another gulping swallow, two deep breaths. His lungs burn as if rubbed with liniment, and now his belly begins to hurt so much it forces him to double over.

Macklin gets to the window where he rightens himself by inhaling and exhaling vigorously. He wipes his cold sweat and the surprise of tears away. All that's left of Sandy is a hollowed-out shell where a trail of wires and tubes intersect: There is nothing there. Nothing is left for Macklin to attach to.

"Goodbye Sandy." Macklin whispers but not to the tangle on the bed. Macklin looks out through the thick double-glazed glass, "Goodbye."

~

"I have to know," Jerry presses Macklin. "You have to decide now, Mack."

"How can I decide?" Macklin looks at Wesley and then at Jerry.

Wesley is stranded on an island of floor between Macklin and Jerry.

Mr. Lu returns.

Mr. Lu's shoulders are stooped. His face is wet with tears.

"Look, Mr. Lu, look!" Wesley scampers to the end table to

fetch his completed collection of vegetable pictures.

"Wes," Jerry calls softly, "not now."

Wesley follows Mr. Lu to the coat rack, "Will you grow a garden next summer, Mr. Lu?" Wesley clings to Mr. Lu's coat sleeve. His voice breaks, "Will you?"

Mr. Lu slowly puts on his coat.

Wesley backs away. Tears are streaming down his face.

Mr. Lu considers his hat for a long while before putting it on.

"Yes. I will grow a garden," Mr. Lu says.

"And I will come and help you," Wesley says solemnly.

"It is many many hard work," Mr. Lu says. "Are you sure you will help me?"

"Yes," Wesley holds out his hand. He and Mr. Lu shake on it.

Mr. Lu nod-bows to Jerry and says to everyone and himself as he leaves. "Yes, I will grow a garden. It is enough, for me, to see things grow."

F.B. André was born in Trinidad, West Indies. He immigrated to Canada in 1971. He lived in Hamilton, Ontario, before moving to Edmonton, Alberta in 1981, and to British Columbia in 1990. Self-employed for the last dozen years, André has held many diverse jobs, including, bartender, gold-miner, factory worker, bookstore clerk, and program administrator, all of which have influenced his writing. André currently lives in Victoria, British Columbia. *The Man Who Beat the Man* is his first book.

CHORUS OF MUSHROOMS
Hiromi Goto

Three generations of Japanese women in small town Alberta find magic and empowerment in sharing stories.

"…a love for words is evident in Chorus of Mushrooms, which contains passages of breathtaking beauty."
—THE GLOBE AND MAIL

ISBN 0-920897-53-3 PB
$14.95 CDN • $10.95 US

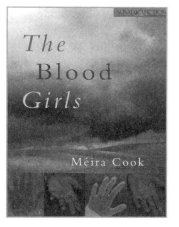

THE BLOOD GIRLS
Méira Cook

Days before Easter in a small Manitoba town, little Donna Desjardins begins bleeding from her palms, then the soles of her feet, and then around the crown of her head.

"Those unfamiliar with this emerging writer have a great read in store."
—CALGARY HERALD

ISBN 1-896300-28-6 PB
$16.95 CDN • $12.95 US

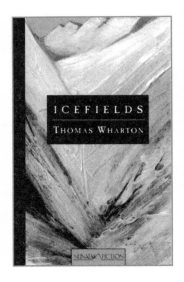

ICEFIELDS
Thomas Wharton

An unusual accident of a glacier in the Rocky Mountains draws an English doctor into the life of the tiny community of Jasper, Alberta as it is transformed from a place of myth and legend into a modern tourist town.

"Ice, when touched, can sear the flesh; in Icefields *it fires the imagination."*
—PEOPLE MAGAZINE

ISBN 0-920897-87-8 PB
$16.95 CDN

MOON HONEY
Suzette Mayr

A funny, sexy tale of love affairs, magical transformation, and happy endings. The question is, can love be relied on to save the day?

ISBN 1-896300-00-6 PB
$14.95 CDN